THE JUNIOR NOVEL

TWENTIETH CENTURY FOX PRESENTS IN ASSOCIATION WITH MARVEL ENTERPRISES, INC. A 1492/BERND EICHINGER PRODUCTION IN ASSOCIATION WITH CONSTANTIN FILM "FANTASTIC FOUR" IOAN GRUFFUDD JESSICA ALBA CHRIS EVANS MICHAEL CHIKLIS JULIAN McMAHON KERRY WASHINGTON MUSIC BY JOHN OTTMAN MUSIC SUPERVISOR DAVE JORDAN FILM EDITOR WILLIAM HOY, A.C.E. PRODUCTION DESIGNER BILL BOES DIRECTOR OF PHOTOGRAPHY OLIVER WOOD EXECUTIVE PRODUCERS STAN LEE KEVIN FEIGE PRODUCED BY CHRIS COLUMBUS BERND EICHINGER AVI ARAD RALPH WINTER MARVEL 1492 PICTURES WRITTEN BY MARK FROST AND SIMON KINBERG AND MIKE FRANCE DIRECTED BY TIM STORY

www.fantasticfourmovie.com

THE JUNIOR NOVEL

ADAPTED BY STEPHEN D. SULLIVAN
BASED ON THE MOTION PICTURE WRITTEN BY
MARK FROST AND SIMON KINBERG
AND MICHAEL FRANCE

HarperKidsEntertainment
An Imprint of HarperCollinsPublishers

CHAPTER 1

DR. REED RICHARDS looked up at the massive metal statue in front of Von Doom Industries headquarters. The statue loomed over the grounds, its unseeing eyes fixed on a triumphant future. Its face was almost as familiar to Reed Richards as his own. It was billionaire Victor Von Doom, Reed's college roommate.

The two of them had studied science together; both were gifted and brilliant. But while Victor had gone on to become a wealthy captain of industry, Reed finished his doctorate and dedicated himself to scientific research. Fortune had not been as kind to Dr. Richards as it had been to his friend. As he gazed up at the statue, Reed cringed at the thought that he was coming to his old roommate looking for help, but what other choice did he have?

Reed and former NASA test pilot Ben Grimm, Reed's

5

best friend, ambled past the statue into the entrance of Von Doom Towers. Ben pulled open the door to the atrium of the soaring, glass-walled building.

"High open space," Reed noted analytically. "Exposed structural elements. Obviously aimed at first-time visitors — to create a feeling of smallness, inadequacy."

Ben Grimm glanced at his friend. "Good thing it ain't workin'," he said. He looked around at the immense building and threw up his oversized hands. "Reed, what are we doing here? This guy's fast-food, strip-mall science. . . ."

Reed sighed. "This *wasn't* our first stop, in case you've forgotten. And Victor's not that bad, he's just a little . . . ," he glanced back at the statue, ". . . larger than life. He's financed some of the biggest scientific breakthroughs of this century."

"Really?" Ben asked sarcastically. "You'd never know it." He gestured toward a number of models and exhibits in the atrium: a clean, safe nuclear facility, the first private space station, and many others. All the displays featured pictures of Victor Von Doom standing front and center.

Reed paused at the reception desk to pick up their building passes.

"Reed Richards and Ben Grimm to see…," Reed began.

The receptionist cut him off. "Executive elevator," she said.

"Top floor." She handed Reed and Ben their clip-on badges.

"Top floor. What a surprise," Ben muttered under his breath.

Reed tucked the small black box he'd brought with him under his arm, and they headed for the elevators.

The executive elevator looked like a combination of security vault and glass skybox. The two men stepped inside and flashed their admission badges in front of the elevator's scanner.

As the elevator rose, Reed fiddled with his necktie.

"Tie that thing any tighter, you're gonna hang yourself," Ben said. "Why are you so nervous? You ran circles around this guy your whole life. What's he got that you don't?"

"A billion dollars and his own space shuttle," Reed replied.

"I mean, other than that," Ben said.

Ben leaned back on Von Doom's leather couch and yawned as Reed adjusted his hologram projector and began his presentation. Bright stars and planets flitted around the darkened room, illustrating Reed's points as he talked.

"My research suggests," Dr. Richards said, "that exposure to a high-energy cosmic storm might have triggered the evolution of early life on earth." He glanced from his presentation to the shadowy figure seated behind a desk on the far side of the room. Victor Von Doom showed little sign of interest.

Reed continued. "In six weeks, another cloud of geomagnetic particles with the same elemental profile will pass earth's orbit. Studying its effects on DNA could fundamentally advance our knowledge about the structure of the human genome, the cause of countless diseases, and . . ."

Von Doom's deep voice pierced the darkness. "Turn it off, please," he said.

Reed sighed and clicked the OFF button on the remote for his hologram projector. "I don't think I've explained my proposal . . ."

Von Doom cut him off. "No," he said. "I think you've explained it perfectly well. Imagination, creativity, passion . . . those were always your trademarks."

The lights in the room came up, revealing the handsome face belonging to the voice. Victor Von Doom stepped from behind his desk and adjusted his perfectly cut twenty-thousand-dollar suit. In his hand, he held a high-tech magazine.

He dropped it on a coffee table next to Reed. The headline on the cover read, "Richards Bankrupt."

"But dreams don't pay the bills, do they?" Victor asked.

"Same old Reed, always stretching, always reaching for the stars."

"Exactly," Reed said, ignoring Victor's dig. "You remember back in school we talked about working together?" He pressed the remote and as the lights dimmed another hologram appeared: a space shuttle slowly approaching an orbiting space station. Both the ship and the station bore the Von Doom Industries logo.

Victor smiled, intrigued. "So, it's not just my money you want," he said. "It's my toys. Tell me, if NASA doesn't trust you, why should I?"

Reed paused, startled that Victor knew about his failure with NASA. Ben sat up on the couch, wide awake. His eyes narrowed as he regarded Victor suspiciously.

Von Doom smiled at their discomfort. "It's my job to stay one step ahead—to know things that other people don't."

Ben rose and walked over to Reed. "Come on," he whispered. "We don't need this."

"Ben," Reed said quietly, "this is business. It's just work."

Victor looked at the two men, seemingly enjoying the tension between them. As he did, a melodious female voice drifted out of one of the room's dark corners.

"You haven't changed, have you, Reed?" the woman said.

Reed and Ben turned and saw Sue Storm standing by the

wall, nearly hidden in the shadows. She'd been watching the whole presentation, practically invisible in the corner.

Sue was beautiful and impeccably dressed, but a touch of resentment marred her face. "Isn't it *always* just work?" she asked.

Victor smiled at her and nodded to Ben and Reed. "I think both of you know my director of genetic research, Susan Storm," he said.

"Hiya, Suzie," Ben said. "Long time, no see." Then, quietly to Reed, he added, "One *more* thing Von Doom's got."

Reed adjusted his necktie.

Sue crossed the room and gave Ben a warm hug. "It's been *too* long," she said.

She politely shook Reed's hand.

"How have you been?" he asked.

"Never better," she replied.

Victor put his hand protectively on her shoulder. "You're just in time to hear the great Dr. Richards ask me for help," he told her. Then to Reed, he said, "You know, you made a lot of folks at MIT feel like they belonged in a junior high science fair. So, you'll excuse me if I savor the moment. Go ahead, Reed. Let's hear it."

Ben clenched his fists as Reed took a deep breath.

"If you back this mission," Reed began, "I'll sign over a fair percentage of any applications . . ."

"The number is *seventy-five*," Victor said. "Seventy-five percent of all applications and patents." He smiled predatorily. "Come on. Twenty-five percent of a billion is still enough to keep the lights on at the Baxter Building for a while, isn't it? Maybe you can even pay off your *fourth* mortgage."

Reed's mouth stretched into a thin line.

"So, what do you say?" Victor asked. "We got a deal?"

Reed looked at Ben. The astronaut shook his head no, just slightly. Reed looked back at Von Doom. Reluctantly, he nodded.

Victor smiled and extended his hand. "Well, then, to our future. Together," he said. Reed took his hand and Von Doom squeezed it, hard.

"Funny how things turn out, isn't it?" Victor said.

"Hilarious," Reed replied. He glanced at Sue, but she avoided his gaze.

Standing nearby, Ben frowned.

CHAPTER 2

AS VICTOR VON DOOM left the meeting room, Leonard, his director of communications, appeared at his side.

"Four weeks before the company goes public," Leonard reminded him.

"If Richards is right," Victor said, "this little trip will double the value of our stock."

"And if he's *not* right?" Leonard asked.

"Reed is *always* right," Victor said enviously.

Back in the meeting room, Ben and Reed headed to the elevator.

"Reed," Ben whispered, "he *knew* about NASA. What if he urged them to shut us down?"

"We got what we wanted," Reed said stiffly.

"I know, I know," the test pilot replied. "I'm just worried about what he really wants. Speaking of which . . ."

His eyes drifted to Sue as she joined them in the elevator.

The doors hissed shut behind her.

"Reed, our readings indicate those solar winds are picking up speed," she said.

"I factored that into my coordinates," Reed replied.

"Of course you did," she shot back. "In *theory*. But things are a little different up there. That's *real* outer space, not some laboratory simulation."

Reed's reply caught in his throat. Somehow, he always felt tied in knots in Sue's presence.

Ben rubbed his big hands together. "I can't wait," he said. "When do we leave?"

"I'll schedule the launch," Sue said. "Call me in the morning to talk about resources and crew." She took a business card out of her suit pocket and extended it to Reed.

"I think I remember the number," he said.

She looked at him coldly. "It's been changed."

Ben winced. Reed took the card. The elevator doors opened onto the main floor.

"As far as crew," Reed said, "I was hoping Ben could pilot the mission. . . ."

"Well," Sue replied, "he's welcome to ride shotgun, but we already have a pilot on our payroll." Turning to Ben, she asked, "You remember my brother, Johnny, don't you?"

Ben nodded and forced a smile through his clenched teeth.

The forest surrounding the Von Doom launch facility stretched to the distant mountains. At the compound's center waited Victor's shuttle—a sleek, ultramodern spacecraft. Its nose pointed straight up toward space. Dozens of workers in Von Doom Industries jumpsuits scampered across the two-hundred-foot-tall scaffolding supporting the ship.

Ben and Reed gazed up at the spacecraft.

"I can't do it," Ben said. "I *cannot* do it."

Reed was surprised. "Two external rocket boosters," he pointed out. "Orbital system engines on either side of the tail. It's just like the shuttles you flew . . ."

"No," Ben insisted. "I cannot take orders from Johnny Storm. I don't care if he *is* Sue's brother. I kicked that wingnut out of NASA for sneaking two models into a flight simulator."

"Johnny was always given to youthful high spirits," Reed said, making the understatement of the century.

"They *crashed* it into a wall," Ben exploded. "They crashed a *flight simulator*. That's not even supposed to be possible."

"I'm sure he's matured since then," Reed responded, barely suppressing a smile.

Just then, a young man on a souped-up motorcycle pulled down the driveway to the launch site. As he drove, he leaned over to kiss a redhead in a flame-colored convertible sports car. It was a ridiculous stunt, but he managed to pull it off.

Ben glared at the motorcycle rider, recognizing Johnny Storm immediately.

"When have I ever asked you to do something you said you absolutely could not do?" Reed asked Ben.

"Five times," Ben replied.

"I had it at four," Reed said.

"This makes five."

The two of them trudged from the launch area back to the locker room to prepare for the trip.

As they packed their gear, a voice announced, "Captain on the bridge!"

Ben instinctively snapped to attention. Johnny Storm strode in and snapped Ben's picture with a digital camera. The twentysomething hotshot had announced *himself* before entering.

He smirked at Ben and said, "Digital camera: two hundred forty-five dollars. Memory stick: fifty-nine dollars. The look on your tough-guy former commanding officer's face when he finds out he's acting as junior copilot to you: priceless."

Ben reached over as if to grab him. Johnny flinched, but Ben merely adjusted the Von Doom Industries logo pin on the front of the youngster's blue formfitting pilot uniform. Ben grinned and turned back to Reed.

"I can handle the borrowed ship," Ben said. "I can even handle Mr. Blond Ambition here. But these space suits they're bringing us . . . I don't know if I should be flying or doing dinner theater in them. Who came up with that bright idea?" He looked dubiously at Johnny's ensemble.

"I did," Susan Storm said as she entered the room. She, too, was clad in a blue wet suit–like uniform. In her hands she held identical sets of clothes for Reed and Ben.

"You might be nostalgic for the fat and baggy look, Ben," she continued, "but the synthetics in these suits act like a second skin, adapting to your individual needs to . . ."

"Keep the hot side hot, and the cool side cool," Johnny said, breaking in.

"Wow," Reed said, checking out Sue's outfit. "Fantastic." He ran his analytical eyes over the uniform she handed him. "Material made from self-regulating unstable molecules. I've been working on a formula for this."

"Great minds think alike," Sue said.

"Some just think faster than others," Victor Von Doom added, as he entered the room. He smiled, looking very dapper in his personally tailored flight suit. "I hired Armani to design the patterns. These colors look great on camera."

"Camera?" Ben asked.

Just then, the door opened and Victor's director of communications, Leonard, entered. "The media is ready for you, sir," he said.

Victor interlaced his fingers and stretched them out in front of him, cracking his knuckles. He smiled. "Showtime," he said, and followed Leonard out the door.

"The rest of you should get to your launch seats," Leonard said. "Mr. Von Doom will join you shortly—after the press conference." He turned and followed his boss out.

"Yeah," Ben said. "No sense sharing any of the glory."

Leonard led Victor down the chrome-plated hallway toward the press room. Von Doom checked his reflection as he walked. He adjusted his uniform and fussed with his hair.

"Our estimated stock numbers are through the roof," Leonard said. "It'll be one of the biggest initial public offerings ever."

"And the launch is going out live?" Victor asked.

"Cable across the board, sir," Leonard said. "Just like you wanted. Network coverage at six, Eastern."

They approached a set of large double doors at the far end of the hallway. Victor stopped and looked at himself one last time in one of the mirrored metal panels.

"Leonard," he said, "does my hair look a little flat?"

Leonard shook his head and smiled.

Victor opened the doors and entered the makeshift pressroom.

The flash of press cameras filled the converted shuttle hangar with light as Victor strode inside. He mounted the steps of a small stage and stood behind a polished steel podium. The press corps waited on the floor below, gazing up at Victor's smiling face.

"Today, we stand on the edge of a new frontier," he began. "In the furthest depths of outer space we will find the secrets to *inner* space. The final key to unlocking our genetic code lies in a cosmic storm . . ."

As he spoke, Reed, Ben, Johnny, and Sue walked past him onto the launch pad. The press corps didn't notice them.

"Isn't that *your* speech?" Ben asked Reed.

Reed nodded. "Yes. He's embellishing it a little."

Ben frowned. Von Doom had trumped Reed again.

The four walked into the ready room beyond the hangar. Waiting there stood a woman in a pink dress with wavy blond hair. She smiled brightly at Ben.

He gave her a hug and kiss. "Debbie, babe," he said. "I am so glad to see you."

"Looks like the big ape's human after all," Johnny muttered.

Debbie slipped a photo of herself into Ben's flight suit. The big test pilot smiled. "I'll be watching over you," he said.

"Just get back soon, or I start looking for a new groom,"

Debbie joked. She fiddled absentmindedly with the engagement ring on her finger.

"As soon as I'm back," Ben said, "I'm gonna trade that in for a bigger rock."

"I don't care about rocks," she said. "I care about you." She turned to Reed and added, "You bring him back in one piece, or you can forget being best man."

Reed smiled and nodded.

Debbie pushed Ben playfully toward the door. "Now go on, get outta here. You know how I hate long good-byes."

Ben gave her another brief kiss and headed for the door. Johnny grinned at him as he went past.

"What are you smilin' at, hotshot?" Ben asked.

Reed, Johnny, and Sue followed him out.

Victor stared confidently into the TV cameras as he wrapped up his press conference.

"Only in America could a country boy from Latveria build one of the biggest corporations in the world," Victor said, "and afford himself the opportunity to reach for the stars."

On a big video screen behind him, steam billowed from the shuttle's engines. The spacecraft was nearly ready to lift off.

Victor smiled magnanimously. "Now if you'll excuse me," he said, "history awaits."

CHAPTER 3

THE VON DOOM INDUSTRIES shuttle split the sky with a deafening sonic boom as it streaked high into the atmosphere.

At the edge of space, the booster rockets detached and the spacecraft fired its main thrusters, arcing away from the blue-green earth.

In the distance, a spinning, wheel-like space station hung in the night-black sky. Stars reflected off the station's polished metal surface. Gigantic VDI logos decorated the station's sides and hub.

Inside the shuttle, Johnny Storm was addressing the crew. "Fasten your seat belts and recline your chairs, lady and gents. We'll be docking in just a few moments." He called up a holographic navigation display and eased the spaceship into the bay at the station's hub.

Victor and Sue led the others into the station.

On their way out, Johnny couldn't resist taunting Ben, "If you behave, next time you can ride up front with the adults."

"Tell me, kid," Ben shot back, "what do you want to be *if* you grow up?"

Feeling reflective, Reed paused by a station window and gazed out into the darkness. Far below, the earth glowed against the glistening stars.

"It's a long way from the projection booth in the Hayden Planetarium, isn't it?" Sue said, coming up behind him.

Reed turned and smiled. It had been a long time since she'd been nice to him. "Yes," he said. "Yes, it is."

"ETA until cosmic event, two hours and counting," Victor announced, cutting short the moment.

He motioned for Sue, Reed, and the rest to keep moving. Sue blushed slightly as Victor led the way to the station's core.

The command center was huge and impressive. Banks of computer controls lined the room's upper deck. The lower level served as an observation room, although closed metal shutters were now covering the floor-to-ceiling windows.

Victor went to a computer console and punched in his access code. "Leonard," he said, "how's the feed?"

Leonard's voice came from a speaker on the console. "Recording, sir. We can see you perfectly." Victor smiled for the camera mounted nearby.

"We can monitor the cloud's approach and observe the tests from here," Sue told Reed and the others.

"My shielding panels are installed?" Reed asked.

"Exactly to your specifications," she replied. "Once these doors seal, we should be completely protected from the cloud's radiation."

"*Should* be?" Ben asked.

"Let's start loading those samples," Reed said.

"Go ahead," Victor agreed. "I need to borrow Susan for a second."

Reed glanced at Sue, but she avoided his gaze. "Sure," he said.

A few minutes later, Johnny and Ben met in the air lock as Reed installed some of his equipment in another part of the station. Ben prepped for a space walk while the younger pilot carefully placed experimental plants, each sealed in a clear box, onto a shelf in the air lock bay.

Johnny shook his head and gave Ben a wry look. "Please tell me the old man's not trying to rekindle things with my sister," he said.

Ben continued fastening his space boots. "'Course not," he replied. "Strictly business."

"Yeah, well, his eyes say different," Johnny countered.

"Hey," Ben snapped, "*two* hearts got busted last time, junior. Maybe *she's* not over it, either."

Johnny rubbed his chin theatrically and stared at the ceiling as though he were thinking hard. "Let's see . . . you've got Victor, stud of the year, more coin than God . . . or Reed, the world's dumbest smart guy who's worth less than a postage stamp. Hmmm . . . I guess it's a toss-up."

"Thinking never was your strong suit," Ben noted.

"Said the *copilot* in training," Johnny replied. "Be careful not to float away, gruesome." He stepped through the air lock door and back into the station, as Ben finished adjusting his space suit.

The young flight commander sealed the air lock and then gazed through the small window set into the door. Ben gave him a thumbs-up. The outer air lock door slid open, and Ben Grimm stepped gracefully out into space.

Sue followed Victor down to the observation deck.

"Surprised I agreed to Reed's proposal?" Victor asked.

"I understand the business reasons," she replied.

"Additionally," Victor said, "when looking at your future, it never hurts to close out your past."

Sue looked at him questioningly.

"Susan," he continued, "every man dreams that he'll meet a woman he can give the world to."

He pressed a button on one of the consoles, and the shields rolled back from the observation deck's outer windows.

Beyond, the blue-green earth hung like a midsummer full moon in the starry sky. The sight was stunningly beautiful.

"In my case," Victor finished, "giving someone the world is not just a metaphor."

Sue gazed out the window, spellbound. She'd been to the station before, but she'd never seen it like this. The scientific part of her brain noted that Victor must have adjusted the station's orbit to show the earth to her. That made her a bit uncomfortable.

She didn't notice as Victor reached into a pocket of his space suit and withdrew a small ring box.

Reed checked data at a workstation in a nearby corridor. He felt puzzled. The sensor readings were not the same as his projections—something that almost never happened.

As he tried to reconcile the two sets of data, the solar wind readouts suddenly shot upward. Sweat beaded on Reed's forehead. He punched the keys of the workstation, inputting new formulas to recheck his calculations.

A cold chill shot up his spine. "No," he said. "No. That's impossible."

The readout before him read: Event Threshold, T-Minus 10:00 minutes.

As another bead of sweat trickled down Reed's brow, the clock started ticking down: 9:59 . . . 9:58 . . .

Victor clutched the engagement ring box behind his back. He took a deep breath.

"You've been with me two years now," he said to Sue.

She nodded. "It's been a good two years, Victor," she said cautiously. "The company's accomplished so much."

"Yes," Victor said, "the *company*. But, Sue, I've come to realize that all the accomplishments in the world mean nothing without someone to share them with."

Sue looked away, turning back to the window. Her body tensed.

"Victor," she said, "I don't think this is the best time."

He stepped forward and continued, used to getting what he wanted.

"I've lived my life unafraid of taking big steps," he said. "Now it's time for the biggest step of all. I have four words, four little words, that can change our lives forever."

He squeezed the ring box and took a deep breath, preparing to show it to her. As he did, the doors to the command center hissed open and Reed rushed into the room.

"The cloud is accelerating!" Reed announced breathlessly.

Von Doom tucked the ring back into his pocket.

"We've got *minutes* until it hits, not hours," Reed said. "We have to abort the experiments!" He leaned up against the wall of the control room, his head reeling. "I don't know what happened. My numbers were . . . wrong."

Sue went to a nearby control panel and punched in some numbers. The readouts confirmed Reed's claim. She nodded to Victor.

Von Doom shrugged. "First time for everything," he said. "Get a grip, Reed. We didn't come all this way to lose our nerve at the first glitch."

"We need to get Ben inside," Reed said.

"So, reel him back in," Victor replied. "But we came here to do a job, so let's do it *quickly*."

Outside the space station, Ben carefully arranged the sealed containers holding Reed's botanical samples into a testing tray. The transparent boxes protected the plants from airless space, but what effect the cosmic storm might have on them . . . well, of all the people in the world, only Reed was smart enough to have even a guess.

Ben shook his head as he worked at arranging the plant samples on his space walk. How could Reed be so brilliant at science and so clueless about human relationships? If Reed had any sense, he never would have let Sue Storm go.

Reed's voice crackled over his radio headset, startling the astronaut. "Ben," Reed said, "we need you back inside. Pronto."

Ben turned toward the station and saw Reed and Johnny staring out a window at him. They looked worried.

"I ain't done arranging your flowers yet, egghead," Ben replied. The main part of the station wouldn't have been far from him on earth, but for a space walk it was a difficult haul. Ben didn't want to have to make the trip twice. Plus, walking in space was dangerous, even though Ben had done it many times before.

"Don't worry about the experiments," Reed said. "Just get back inside."

"If you don't," Johnny added, "you'll be *done* for sure. Look behind you, you big ape." He pointed off, into space.

Ben turned and looked.

In the distance, the cosmic storm roiled, like a typhoon building at sea. It was blue and purple and red, with misty tendrils and boiling clouds. Cosmic lightning flashed within its depths. It would have seemed beautiful, but Ben knew the danger it held.

"Roger that," he said to the others. "I'm on my way."

He turned and headed for the ship, wishing he could move faster. But the bulky space suit made that impossible. Even worse, any small slip and he'd lose his grip on the station and float away into space. Then it wouldn't matter if the cosmic storm caught him or not. Either way, he'd be dead.

CHAPTER 4

VICTOR GAZED AT THE MONITORS in the command center. He watched Johnny and Reed, clustered near the main air lock, waiting for Ben. Another monitor showed the cosmic storm approaching the station. The flashing, swirling cloud raced forward, far faster than Victor would have believed possible.

Sue watched the sensor monitors on a console nearby.

The automated voice of the station's warning system announced, "Event threshold in two minutes."

A trickle of sweat ran down Victor's cheek.

Reed and Johnny stood by the air lock door, both urging Ben to move faster, but there was nothing they could do. Slowly, methodically, Ben made his way back toward the station. Behind him, the storm grew larger by the second, pushing waves of pressure ahead of it.

"It's accelerating," Reed said.

Victor's voice crackled over the radio link. "Reed," he said, "we're running out of time."

"Come on, big guy," Johnny whispered. "You can do it."

Outside, the first wave of the cloud's outer layer hit Ben. The veteran astronaut struggled to keep his grip. He forced his legs forward, even as the turbulence tried to rip him from the station's surface.

The station shook with the storm's first impact.

Tendrils of misty energy reached from the cloud toward Ben. The station air lock lay ahead of him, only twenty yards away. Yet every step seemed to take a lifetime.

Victor paced the control room, trying hard not to sweat, or—at least—not to let Sue see him sweat. He almost pushed her aside as he stabbed the intercom button with his finger. "Reed, you need to get up here so we can close the shields. Now!" His voice was cold, commanding.

Sue glared at him, startled by his lack of compassion.

"Not until Ben is back inside," Reed replied.

"It's too late for him," Victor said. "And soon, it'll be too late for all of us." Not waiting for Reed's reply, he moved to the command console and began punching keys.

"What are you doing?" Sue asked.

Victor didn't even look at her. "Raising the shields."

"You *can't* leave them there," Sue said.

"Watch me," Victor shot back.

Sue was furious. She took a step toward the control room door, then glanced back at him.

"Don't be stupid, Sue," Victor said. "No sense throwing your life away to uphold some naive notion of solidarity among comrades. You can't help them any more than I can."

"I can try," Sue said, determined. With one final, angry glare at her boss, she ran out of the room.

Victor watched the shields slide down around him, sealing him, alone, in the control room.

Meanwhile, Sue dashed down the hallway toward the air lock, determined to reach her brother, Reed, and Ben.

Reed bit his lip and looked at Johnny, standing beside him. If they stayed here, by the air lock, all of them would probably die.

"Victor's right," Reed said. "Johnny, get to the command center. Close the shields."

"What about you?" Johnny asked. He saw the answer in the scientist's face. Reed would not leave without Ben. Johnny steeled his courage. He wasn't about to leave, either.

"Come on, big guy!" he shouted to Ben. "You can do it!"

The automated warning system announced, "Event threshold in thirty seconds."

Ben punched the keypad outside and the exterior door of the air lock slid open. Weightlessness made everything move in agonizing slow motion, and it took forever for Ben to pull himself inside.

Before Ben could haul himself completely inside and seal the door behind him, the full force of the cosmic storm hit.

A hissing mass of space dust pelted Ben's body, spattering his space suit with sandy orange particles, while larger pieces of storm debris and small burning stones buffeted him.

He reached for the door controls, but they remained just beyond his fingertips.

"Event threshold in ten seconds," the metallic voice of the space station announced. "Nine . . . eight . . ."

As soon as Ben was far enough inside, Johnny punched the interior control panel and the air lock door began to close behind Ben.

Reed grabbed a thermoelastic blanket from a first aid kit, ready to help Ben when the air lock cycled and the inner door opened.

Sue rounded the corner nearest Reed and her brother. "Johnny! Reed!" she called.

The computer voice kept counting. "Five . . . *four* . . ."

The station quaked as the storm hit it with full force.

Alone inside the control room, Victor stood defiantly. He clutched the diamond ring in his hand, unaware he held it. His eyes examined the storm on the video monitors with the cold detachment of a scientist.

Everywhere wires sparked and lights exploded. Equipment shook loose and fell around him. Victor ignored the chaos and glanced down at the sensor readouts, looking to gauge the storm's fury.

As he did, the control panel exploded in his face.

Victor staggered back into the falling equipment. The panel he stumbled against gave way and collapsed under his weight. Sparking debris fell from the ceiling, burying him.

The outer air lock door closed far too slowly. Particles from the storm streamed inside, tearing into Ben. He screamed in pain as the glowing space dust burned into his skin. He inched toward the inner door, trying to escape.

Chaos reined inside the space station.

Reed grabbed for the inner air lock door, trying to help his friend, but the door remained just out of reach. He stretched for it with all his might.

The door's control panel caught fire, showering Johnny

with sparks. Johnny staggered back, trying to tamp out the flames with his hands.

Overhead, an air conduit burst, spraying Sue with cold steam. She reeled, unable to see anything.

With a final lurch, the outer door slid shut and sealed itself just as a flaming cosmic particle ripped through the back of Ben's suit. Ben collapsed against the inner door.

The space station shuddered, and everything went dark.

CHAPTER 5

SILENCE FILLED THE LIGHTLESS space station. Their backup power systems clicked on, and with a reassuring hum, the station sprang back to life.

Victor crawled out from under the rubble within the command center.

He stood and looked himself over: a few scrapes and bruises but nothing serious, aside from a nasty headache.

He crossed to one of the polished steel wall panels and looked at his reflection. A thin cut, perhaps an inch and a half long, traced down his temple near his left eyebrow.

The wound wasn't bleeding, but it throbbed dully when he touched it. Victor frowned.

He set to work on the damaged control panel and soon had the surveillance system working once more.

The station seemed to be mostly intact. That was good. Perhaps Richards and the others survived the storm as well—even without the benefit of a shield.

Perhaps *Sue* survived.

Victor worked the controls and soon saw the air lock area on the main monitor.

Amid the rubble of the outer ring, Reed and Johnny scrambled to open the air lock's interior door. Sue came to their aid as the door hissed open and Ben toppled out.

The astronaut's spacesuit smoked where the cosmic debris had pelted it. His helmet looked scarred and pitted.

The others pulled Ben out of the air lock, and the door sealed automatically behind them.

Victor wondered detachedly if Ben was still alive.

Reed worked to remove his friend's helmet. "He's not responsive," he told Johnny and Sue.

"Ben!" Johnny shouted. "Ben!"

An unfamiliar darkness surrounded Ben Grimm.

In the distance, a familiar voice called to him.

"Ben, wake up. Wake up!"

Slowly, Ben opened his eyes and Johnny's youthful face blurred into view.

"Where am I?" Ben asked.

"Back on earth," Johnny replied. "In Victor's medical facility. We're in quarantine."

"Reed?" Ben asked. "Sue?"

"They're fine," Johnny said. "Everyone *else* . . . is fine." He turned away from the older astronaut.

Something tightened in Ben's chest. "What's wrong with me?" he asked.

"I swear to you," Johnny said, "they've done everything humanly possible. The best plastic surgeons in the world were here, Ben. You had the best—"

"Give me a mirror."

Johnny grabbed the hand mirror on the bedside table before Ben could pick it up. He seemed reluctant to hand it over. "Ben, they said that's not such a good idea," he said. "The shock alone could . . ."

"Gimme that!" Ben thundered.

He grabbed the mirror from Johnny's hand and raised it to his face.

He looked completely normal, aside from a serious growth of stubble on his chin.

"Unfortunately," Johnny finished his joke, "the doctors just couldn't do anything to fix that ugly mug."

He laughed and headed for the door. Ben heaved the mirror at him. It hit the doorframe, breaking into hundreds of pieces.

Reed wandered the gardens of Victor's modern medical facility, lost in thought. The building was all glass and steel, nestled into a lush green forest. The hospital stood in stark contrast to the natural beauty around it, as if reinforcing humans' dominance over nature.

Reed picked a lily from one of the carefully manicured flower beds and headed back inside. As he did so, he crossed behind a press conference Victor was giving. Reed paused a moment to listen.

For once, the head of Von Doom Industries looked less than perfect. His hair flopped carelessly over his forehead. A bandage covered a small spot over his left brow.

"Danger is always part of discovery," Victor said. "Without risk, there is no reward."

"It seems like your *crew* risked more than you," a reporter commented.

Anger momentarily flashed across Victor's face. Then he said, "Thank God they're safe and sound, resting here, in my personal facility. They've earned a vacation."

"Are you still taking VDI public in . . ."

"Three weeks, yes," Victor said, smiling once more. "I've never been more confident in my company. In fact, I'm putting everything I have into company stock—as a show of support."

Reed ducked inside and went up to Sue's room. She was asleep in bed. A doctor was scribbling notes on her chart.

"How's she doing?" Reed asked.

"Stable," the doctor replied. "Vitals are strong."

Reed took the clipboard and examined it himself. "Blood panels show no irradiation. Good. You'll step up this protocol every—"

The doctor cut him off. "Four hours. We know what we're doing." He took the clipboard and left.

Reed stepped closer to the bed, the drooping lily still in his hand.

"Sue," he said quietly, "I'm sorry. You were right about . . ."

Before he could complete the thought, a nurse rolled in with a huge tray full of extravagant bouquets. Reed glanced at the card: Victor. Of course. He looked down at his own wilting flower, then sighed and headed for the door.

"She's allergic to orchids," Reed called back as he left. "Put that *Amaryllis apapathos* by her bed. African lilies are her favorites."

He dumped his flower in the trash on the way out.

Johnny adjusted the fit of his skiing outfit as the nurse entered his room.

"Where do we think we're going?" the nurse, a cute blonde woman, asked.

"I don't know if *we've* noticed, but the slickest runs

this side of the Alps are right outside that window," Johnny replied.

"I've noticed," the nurse said. "But the doctor said you're not allowed to leave until we—"

He completed her sentence. "Finish the tests, I know. Could you give me a hand with this zipper?"

"This isn't a ski resort," the nurse said.

"Not yet," Johnny replied. He reached under his bed and pulled out a box containing a collapsable snowboard. "Luckily, Grandma sends care packages."

The nurse popped a digital thermometer in his mouth.

"You are trouble," she said.

"Brubble's my triddle name," Johnny mumbled around the thermometer.

The nurse helped him with the zipper on his jacket. "You feel hot," she said.

"I've never felt better in my life," Johnny replied. "When do you get off work?"

"My shift ends in an hour," she replied, "but I couldn't . . ."

"Meet me at four-oh-one at the top of the run," Johnny insisted. "That'll give you a minute to freshen up."

He handed the thermometer back to her and headed out the door. The nurse smiled at him and nodded. Neither of them noticed that Johnny's temperature had registered at 209 degrees.

*　　*　　*

Ben found Reed on a ward patio, overlooking an amazing view of the mountain and ski slope beyond. Reed gazed thoughtfully into the sky, barely noticing Ben's arrival.

"How long was I out?" Ben asked.

"Three days," Reed replied. "How are you feeling?"

"Solid," Ben said. "Reed, what happened up there?"

Reed shook his head. "I don't know. I've never miscalculated like that before."

Ben nodded. "You go through something like this, it really makes you appreciate having the right woman in your life."

"Yeah," Reed agreed. "You and Debbie are perfect."

"Reed, I'm not talking about Debbie. And this *ain't* the first time you miscalculated." He shifted his eyes from the mountains to a patio on the level below.

Reed followed his gaze. On a lower balcony, Sue looked out at the panorama.

"Come on," Reed said. "She's got a good thing with Victor."

"Did that cosmic bath loosen your screws?" Ben asked.

"He's smart, powerful, successful," Reed continued.

"Well, maybe *you* should date him," Ben shot back.

Reed looked wearily at his old friend. "Ben," he said,

"she ended up with the right guy. He'll give her the life she deserves." He turned and left.

Ben fumed. "Do I have to do *everything* myself?"

Johnny stood atop the hill. Below him stretched a death-defying black diamond run. He *lived* for things like this.

His nurse emerged from the ski lodge behind him wearing a bright pink ski outfit. Johnny smiled. He lived for things like her, too.

He dropped his black snowboard with green flames onto the snow at the crest of the run.

The nurse smiled at him. "One thing you should know about this hill," she said. "Stay right. Left is trouble."

Johnny rolled his eyes. "I thought we went over this already," he said.

She shrugged. "Okay, hotshot," she said. "Have it your way." She pulled down her goggles and shoved off, darting quickly down the slope. Clearly she'd been on this trail many times before. Johnny knew he'd have to work hard to stay with her.

Johnny felt hot under the collar of his ski suit. He took a deep breath, leaped onto his board, and took off down the slope.

When she zigged, he zagged, soaring over treacherous

moguls, steadily closing the distance between them. He craved speed, willing himself forward, pushing himself to become a human rocket.

His ski cap fell off. His lungs burned within him. It felt as though flames were lapping at his hair. He smiled as he finally drew even with the nurse.

"You're on fire!" the nurse called.

"Hey, thanks!" Johnny called back. "You're pretty hot yourself."

"No!" she cried. "I mean you're *on fire!*"

CHAPTER 6

JOHNNY LOOKED DOWN at his hands. His gloves were burning with bright orange flames.

Frantically, he jerked them off and tossed them aside.

He glanced behind and watched the gloves sizzle out in the snow. But now his back was on fire, too!

Stress and anxiety shot through him. His body shuddered, and suddenly he shot forward, as though propelled by jets.

The nurse gaped and lost her concentration. Her skis splayed out from under her, and she fell into the snow.

Johnny kept going, rocketing down the slope at a frightening velocity. He tried to rip off his flaming jacket, but in doing so veered to the left.

Trees shot by and the ground fell away beneath his board.

Johnny screamed as he flew off the snow-covered edge of a huge cliff.

He flailed his arms and legs, trying to catch onto something, but there was nothing to catch onto.

Fire covered his body as he plummeted, turning everything around him a shade of the most intense orange. He became a blazing human torch, falling to his death.

The rocks rushed up at him.

The fire burned more brightly. Johnny knew he was about to die. He tried to stop falling, knowing it was futile. Then, without warning, he *did* stop. And not with the bone-crushing impact he expected.

For a moment, his blazing body hung in the air over the deadly rocks. He angled away from them, like a skydiver controlling his fall. He glanced back at jagged outcrop, unable to believe his luck.

As he did, he crashed hard into a deep snowbank.

The snow instantly extinguished his flames. Cold white powder surrounded him completely, filling his mouth and eyes, crushing down on him. He flailed at the snow, trying to dig his way out, but it was no use. Panic rose up in him again.

He sweated and his body felt hot, very hot. He burst into flame once more. The snow around him melted rapidly. The flames died away again, and he found himself sitting in a puddle as deep as a hot tub. Steam rose from the newly melted water.

The nurse, who had recovered from her fall, skied down to him. She looked astonished to find him alive.

He smiled and sat back in the steaming pool he had created. "Care to join me?" he asked.

Victor paced atop the parapet of his medical center, admiring his billion-dollar view of the nearby mountains. His staff prepared the table in his building-top office for a romantic dinner. They straightened the tablecloth and linen napkins, arranged the antique silverware, and brought out covered dishes of food.

Victor checked everything, every knife and fork, every dish. Leonard followed him around, trying to keep up.

"How are the numbers for tomorrow?" Victor asked.

"Stable," Leonard said. "Which is good, considering the fallout from the space station incident."

"I don't want good," Victor said. "I want *great*. I've got every dollar of my fortune riding on this. Get me on the A.M. shows, and put a couple of cameras on the exchange floor."

Victor lifted a silver tray from the table and gazed at his own reflection in it. His eyes focused on the scar on his brow. "I've got to do something about this scar," he muttered.

"Actually, the scar is tracking well, sir," Leonard said. "People think it humanizes you."

Victor gazed at the scar, at his pale skin, at his bloodshot eyes.

"You should get some rest," Leonard suggested.

"Later," Victor replied. "First I've got some unfinished business—a deal that needs closing."

Leonard glanced at the lavish table setting. "Sir," he said, clearing his throat, "I've always wondered, why *Sue*? You could have any woman in the world, but . . ."

"That's why," Victor interrupted. "Because I could have any *other* woman."

Sue headed toward one of the compound's stylish eateries alongside Ben. "I can only stay for coffee," she told him. "I promised Victor I wouldn't be late."

Ben nodded. "Absolutely."

They rounded a corner into the quiet, dimly lit cafe just as Reed entered by another door.

"Hey, Reed," Ben said. "What are you doing here?" Before Reed could answer, he added, "Great. Why don't you join us?"

Putting his big arms around Reed and Sue, he shepherded them toward a quiet table in the corner of the room. "Boy, I'm starving," Ben said. "Order me a beer, would you? I'm gonna hit the buffet."

Sue and Reed glanced nervously at each other.

They were still looking nervously at each other when Ben finished his huge dinner. He belched. "Pardon me," he said.

Reed and Sue looked at him. His stomach was growling so loudly, they could hear it.

"Are you all right?" Reed asked.

"I think I need to lie down," Ben said. As he got up from the table, his stomach bulged slightly. He groaned and lurched out of the cafe.

Getting ill hadn't been part of his plan, but throwing Sue and Reed together . . . at least that had worked. He glanced back at the two of them, sitting alone in the corner, and smiled.

A waiter placed a lit candle on the table Sue and Reed shared. Sue looked lovely in the candlelight.

"Are you feeling better?" Reed asked.

"Yes," she replied. "Thanks."

"That's good. That's . . . uh . . . good."

Sue frowned. "You always had a way with words." She picked up her coffee and drank the last bit. "I should probably be getting back."

Reed didn't say anything.

Exasperated, Sue stood to go.

Reed tried desperately to think of something, anything,

to say. "I'm really happy for you and Victor," he blurted.

"You're happy for me and Victor," she said, disbelieving. "You're *happy* for us?"

"I can tell you two are enjoying what was the best part of our relationship . . . ," he said, groping for words.

"Which was?" she asked, turning toward the door.

"Passion," he replied.

She stopped, surprised, and sat back down.

"For science," Reed finished.

Sue shook her head. "You are such a jerk, Reed," she said. "You never got it, and you never will unless it's explained to you in binary code." She stared icily at him. The flame on the candle on the table bent sideways and flickered, as if blown by a ghostly breeze.

"What did I say?" Reed asked.

"It's never what you say, Reed," she replied. "It's what you *don't* say. It's what you don't *do.* . . ."

She seemed to want Reed to say something, but he couldn't figure out what.

"I—I just think that you and Victor . . ."

Sue leaned back into the shadows near the wall. Her face flushed.

"At least Victor's not afraid to take a stand and *fight* for what he wants," she said. She sighed, and as she did, she slowly faded into the background.

"It's nice to be wanted sometimes," she continued. "To be heard, and seen . . ." Only her eyes remained now, and the blush on her cheeks. The rest of Sue had become totally invisible.

Reed looked around, near panic. "Sue," he said. "Sue! Where are you?"

"I'm not joking, Reed," she said angrily.

"Neither am I," Reed said. "Sue, look down."

Sue looked down and saw nothing. To all appearances, she wasn't even there.

She shrieked and stood up, bumping into the table. The table tipped precariously and a wine bottle tumbled off.

Instinctively, Reed Richards reached for it. But the bottle was too far, nearly at the floor.

Reed's arm stretched farther than humanly possible and grabbed the bottle before it hit. Reed looked at his arm. It was two feet longer than normal. He had stretched it like a rubber band.

Both Reed and Sue glanced at each other, alarmed.

Just then, Johnny came into the dining hall. "You guys will not believe what just happened to me!" he said.

Victor stared at the flickering candle on his elaborately set table. The candle burned low, almost smothering itself in a pool of its own molten wax. The office was dark now, and the carefully prepared dinner cold.

Victor scowled and fished a cell phone from his pocket.

He punched in Sue's number. The phone rang, but no one answered. Victor waited a few rings, then hung up, frustrated. He squeezed the phone tightly and the impact-resistant case cracked in his grip.

He headed for the door. As he did, he passed a full-length mirror by the doorway. He paused, staring at his reflection. He moved closer, his eyes focused on the bandaged scar on his brow.

The wound looked longer now. It protruded slightly from under the sides of the bandage. And perhaps it was a trick of the light, but the scar appeared bluish-gray, almost metallic.

CHAPTER 7

REED, SUE, AND JOHNNY walked urgently down the hallway toward one of Von Doom's science labs.

"It has to be the cloud," Sue said. "It's fundamentally altered our DNA."

"Let's not jump to conclusions," Reed replied. "We need evidence before making that leap." He glanced over to Johnny, and his jaw dropped.

The young pilot's fingertips were on fire. He snapped his fingers, and the flames went out. He seemed totally unharmed.

"Now, what's up with *that*?" Johnny asked.

"The cloud *has* fundamentally altered our DNA," Reed said, getting all the evidence he needed.

"Cool," Johnny said. "So, what'd it do to you guys?"

"Apparently, I can disappear," Sue said.

"Well, it's about time," Johnny joked.

Reed suddenly looked very worried. "We have to find Ben," he said.

As one, they changed direction and headed for Ben's room.

Johnny snapped his fingers as they walked. Each time he snapped, small bursts of flame formed around his fingertips.

"It's like one of those old commercials," he said. "Flame on . . . Flame off . . . Flame on . . . Flame off . . ."

"Stop," Sue said.

"Flame on . . . Flame off . . ."

"Stop it!" she snapped.

Johnny shrugged at her. "Okay . . . 'Mom.'"

They reached Ben's door. Painful moaning came from inside.

"Ben, are you all right?" Reed called.

The moaning continued.

"Open up, Ben," Sue said. "We need to talk."

"Leave me alone!" someone bellowed from inside. The voice sounded like Ben's, but deeper, more gravely.

Reed tried the door, but it was locked. He kneeled and put his fingers to the crack beneath the door.

"What are you . . . ?" Sue began.

"Quiet, please," Reed said. "I'm not sure this will work. I need to concentrate."

As Sue and Johnny watched, Reed's fingers and hand

stretched and flattened, until his arm could fit under the door. Reed reached in, bent his arm upward, and undid the latch.

Smiling, he pulled his arm back. The arm re-formed, becoming normal once more.

Johnny stared at him. "That is *disgusting!*" the young pilot said.

A huge crash sounded from inside Ben's room.

Sue flung open the door and they all rushed in. Every stick of furniture in the room had been smashed into splinters. A huge hole gaped in the wall where his window used to be.

They ran to the opening and glimpsed a huge, hulking shape running off into the darkness.

"What is that *thing*?" Johnny asked. "Do you think it hurt Ben?"

Sue swallowed hard. "I think that thing *is* Ben."

Reed peered into the darkness, wondering what his experiment had done to his best friend.

Victor appeared in the room's doorway. He paused, surprised by the shambles of the room. He rubbed the bandage on his forehead.

"What's going on?" he asked.

"Victor," Sue said, "are you all right? I mean, physically?"

"Just a couple of scrapes and bruises," he replied. "Why?"

"Ben did this," Reed said. "He's had some kind of reaction to his cosmic storm exposure." He took a deep breath. "And he's not the only one."

"Anybody have an idea where the big lug might be going?" Johnny asked.

Reed nodded. "He's going home."

New York City bustled with nightlife. People streamed down the streets and avenues having dinner, attending plays, visiting nightclubs. There were millions of people in New York, but Ben cared about only one.

Ben parked his "borrowed" Von Doom Industries van behind a Big & Tall men's store. The store was taking a delivery, but no one was working in the truck at the moment. That was good luck; Ben didn't want to be seen.

He went into the vehicle and selected a large trench coat, extra-large gloves, and a fedora hat for himself. He left a big wad of crumpled money to pay for his "purchase" and stalked off into the night.

He headed for his old neighborhood and then found a pay phone.

Ben picked up the phone and looked at the keypad. His gloved fingers were far too large to punch the tiny keys. He tried with no luck for several seconds before finally hitting the "O" key.

"Hello, operator?" he said. "I need you to ring a number for me."

As the operator made the connection, Ben peered up the street toward a modest, working-class home. A light burned in the living room window. Ben's heart nearly melted when he saw Debbie pick up the phone inside.

"Deb," he said, "it's me. I need you to step out back for a minute."

"Out back?" she said. "Are you home, baby? I've got a surprise for you."

Ben blinked back a tear.

"I got a surprise for you, too," he said darkly.

A minute later, Debbie stepped out the back door of her home. She hastily hung a big "Welcome Home" sign over the doorway and then turned to look for Ben. At first, she didn't see him in the darkness.

"Ben . . . ?" she asked.

"Don't come any closer for a sec," he said from the shadows. "This is gonna be kind of a shock." He took a deep breath. "Honey, you remember when we said we'd be together forever, no matter what?"

"Baby, you're scaring me," she said. She clutched her dressing robe tighter around her body.

Ben stepped into the light and removed his disguise.

He was huge, easily twice as bulky as he had once

been. A rocky orange hide, like living armor, covered his entire body. His brow jutted out, overshadowing his blue eyes—the only recognizable thing that remained of the man who had once been Benjamin Grimm.

Debbie gasped. "Oh my g-g-g . . . ! What did you do to Ben?" she asked frantically.

The thing took a hesitating step forward. "Deb, it's me," Ben said. "It's still me."

He reached for her, but she recoiled. Tears sprang to her eyes, and she backed away, sobbing.

He stepped closer. She backed up faster, tripping over her robe and falling into some folding chairs. Ben reached out to help her, but she scuttled away, terrified.

"Don't!" she cried. "Don't touch me!"

Her shouts woke the neighbors. Lights flickered on in the adjoining houses.

Ben looked at her, trembling, terrified. Moisture budded at the corner of his eyes. He knew he had to leave.

"I love you, Deb," he said quietly.

Then he turned and lumbered back into the darkness.

The next day, at the Von Doom compound, Victor was packing his ultraexpensive, monogrammed suitcase. Leonard stood by the door, waiting for instructions.

"Make sure we find Ben," Victor said. "Bring him back here. We can't afford any more problems."

Leonard nodded. "Yes, sir. But we're running late for the stock offering."

"Fine, fine," Victor snapped. "What's our schedule?"

"At nine-thirty you ring the opening bell. We've got two cameras on the floor of the exchange and one in the box. The bank's vice presidents are meeting us there." He smiled. "Today Wall Street, tomorrow . . . who knows? Maybe Washington."

Victor turned to Leonard and frowned. "Leonard," he said, disappointed, "think *bigger*."

The two of them hurried to catch the chopper waiting to take them to the New York.

Ben sat on a girder on the Brooklyn Bridge, staring down at the river. To the cars passing below, he looked like some kind of brooding gargoyle, perched on the steel above. Few people using the bridge gave him a second look.

"In a few days we'll be in space . . . ," he muttered to himself, remembering. "It'll be great. What's the worst that could happen?"

A sobbing sound from nearby distracted him from his own misery. He turned and spotted a businessman with a briefcase standing on the girders nearby. The man held the case out over the water and let it drop. It plunged into the river, hundreds of feet below.

The man steeled himself, preparing to jump.

"You think you got trouble?" Ben rumbled. "Take a good look, pal. How bad could it be?"

The words startled the man. He turned toward Ben, and fear washed over his face. He nearly toppled off the girder. Ben stepped forward to try and help him.

"Okay, easy there, buddy," Ben said.

The man backpedaled, slipped, and fell toward the roadway. He thrashed out with his arms and caught hold of a narrow beam. His fingers gripped the steel tight as his legs dangled over the speeding traffic. Cars and trucks zoomed underneath him, barely missing his feet.

Ben shook his head. "You had to choose my spot to jump, didn't you?" he griped.

He stepped out onto the smaller girder to help, but the beam bent under his weight. The man lost his grip and fell to the road below. He landed during a break in the traffic, but the fall stunned him.

Ben, still on the girder, watched as a huge truck raced across the bridge straight toward the dazed man.

"This really is *not* my day," Ben said.

He hopped off the beam and landed next to the businessman with a bridge-shaking *thud!* He scooped up the stunned man as the truck bore down on them.

With no time to run, the thing that was Ben Grimm turned his rocky shoulder toward the speeding vehicle, trying to shield the man with his own body.

Ben squeezed his eyes shut and braced for the impact.

CHAPTER 8

THE DRIVER of the eighteen-wheeler spotted the duo and slammed on his brakes. An agonized squeal from the truck's tires split the air. The truck slowed, but not nearly enough. The driver turned the wheel at the last moment, trying to avoid Ben and the businessman. It didn't work.

The huge vehicle slammed full force into Ben's rocky shoulder.

The truck stopped as though it had hit a wall of granite. The front of the eighteen-wheeler buckled, crumpling all the way to the passenger compartment. The driver jerked forward, but his seat belt and air bag kept him from flying through the windshield. The safety glass shattered into a thousand fragments and rained down around Ben's stony body.

The rear of the truck fishtailed into the other lanes of traffic. Cars swerved, tires screeched, and horns blared.

Vehicles slammed into one another, causing a massive traffic accident across all four lanes of the bridge.

Twisted masses of metal blocked the road. Some of the wrecks—including the truck—caught fire.

The last car to slam into the pile was an NYPD patrol cruiser. Two stunned policemen clambered out.

Ben straightened up, shocked but unhurt. The suicidal businessman was also unharmed. Ben looked around at the destruction he and the jumper had inadvertently caused. He couldn't tell right away how many people might have been injured. Moans and screams came from all directions.

The driver of the truck lay pinned in his cab, trapped between burning hunks of twisted metal.

Ben left the jumper and went to help the truck driver. The businessman woozily scrambled to his feet and ran for safety.

Ben slammed his fist into the truck's air bag, popping it like a balloon. He reached past the shattered glass to try and undo the man's seat belt. The remains of the windshield crumbled against Ben's rocky skin.

He fumbled with the belt latch. His transformed fingers were too large to manipulate something so small. Flames licked out of the crushed engine, but Ben's thick hide didn't feel them.

"Hey!" he called to the semiconscious driver. "A little help here? You wanna hit that release button, sir?"

But the driver was too out of it. Ben moved to the side of the cab. The door had been badly crumpled by the accident; its lock and handle were shattered.

Ben dug his fingers into the metal and pulled. The door ripped off like cardboard in his hands. He tossed the wreckage aside and grabbed the driver's seat. Effortlessly he tore the seat, with the man still harnessed to it, from the burning truck.

A grim smile cracked Ben's stony face; perhaps there were advantages to his new body. He turned from the wrecked vehicle to find two of New York's Finest pointing their guns at him.

"Freeze!" the first cop said. "Put the man and the seat down!"

For a moment, Ben couldn't believe what he was hearing. Although he'd been partly responsible for the accident, he'd just saved the lives of two men—the businessman and now the driver.

But the cops weren't the only people alarmed by him. Other people in the area, including other accident victims, stared and pointed. To them, Ben didn't look like a hero, he looked like a rock-covered monster.

Frustration welled up in Ben's heart. No matter how

many lives he saved, to most people he would still only be an ugly, misshapen *thing*.

The traffic jam caused by the accident quickly backed up to the bridge's entrances. Drivers slammed on their brakes, barely missing one another in the confusion. The taxicab containing Reed, Sue, and Johnny almost rear-ended the sports car in front of it.

Reed paid the driver. "Let's go," he said. He could sense the trouble ahead.

The trio got out of the cab and surveyed the scene. Ahead, traffic had ground to a halt. Ben stood in the center of the mess, holding a man in a car seat aloft with one hand. Other accident victims and onlookers kept their distance from the rocky-skinned thing. For the first time, Reed and the rest got a good look at their friend.

"Oh, man!" Johnny said. "That is cruel and unusual."

On the bridge, Ben put the driver and seat down. With amazing speed, he darted behind the crashed truck. The police tried to follow, but the burning wreckage held them back. Ben loped away, keeping his head down. He tried to avoid the onlookers and hide from the pedestrians on the overhead walkways.

A scream from an injured motorist rose over the rest of the chaos. Ben stopped, listened, and then went to help.

Reed, Sue, and Johnny raced through the stopped cars toward the flames. Nearly everyone else headed in the opposite direction, away from the "rampaging monster." More police arrived to herd the remaining onlookers away from the scene of the accident.

The two cops who had initially spotted Ben stopped Reed and the others near the entrance to the bridge's main span.

"Get back," one of the police officers said. "We're evacuating the bridge." They looked very determined.

The trio stopped short. Sue glanced at Reed. "What now, Reed?" she asked.

Reed looked around, unsure of himself.

"Ben's out there," Sue pressed. "Let's go get him."

Despite the police barricade, many people were still trapped in the big traffic jam.

The second cop stepped forward. "Maybe you folks didn't hear us. The cars near that wreck are gonna blow sky-high any second. You need to get out of here. Now."

"There are people out there," Reed said, "and one of them is our friend. He's in trouble. We need to get to him before—"

The cop cut him off. "Nobody gets past this point until the rescue crews arrive. We don't need any more victims. There's nothing you can do to help."

Reed glanced at Sue, winked awkwardly, and nodded toward Ben.

"What?" she asked.

"We need to leave," Reed said. "Like you *left* in the dining hall."

Sue nodded, finally understanding. She, Reed, and Johnny backed away from the police, just slightly.

"I don't even know if it will work again," Sue whispered.

"Try!" Reed urged.

She took a deep breath and concentrated. Nothing happened.

"See," she said. "Nothing! I don't know why I listen to you. You'd think I'd have learned my lesson after all these years . . ."

As her anger built, she quickly faded from view.

The police gasped and drew their guns. By then, nothing remained of Sue. The cops looked around, bewildered.

Sue's invisible hands plucked the weapons out of their grasp and tossed the guns away.

The cops wheeled, confused, looking for their invisible opponent. As they did, Reed and Johnny dashed through the makeshift barricade.

The two men split up, moving to each side of the wreckage, looking for their friend. At first, they couldn't see him through the confused crowd and burning heaps.

Reed stretched his neck up, like a giraffe, to peer over the top of a huge, jackknifed semi. He spotted Ben pulling a victim out of a car on the other side. Crumpled, burning vehicles separated them, but Reed used his newfound powers to stretch around the obstacles.

Finally, he came face-to-face with his old friend.

Ben nearly jumped out of his rocky skin.

"What the . . . ?" he said. The woman he'd just rescued screamed and ran away.

"Ben, are you okay?" Reed asked.

"Am *I* okay?" Ben said. "You wanna explain why you're a human rubber band all of a sudden?" Then he pointed at his own stonelike body. "Or how about explainin' this. What the heck *am* I? 'Cause I sure ain't Ben Grimm anymore."

Reed returned his body to normal. He opened his mouth as if to explain, but words failed him—again.

"Reed! Ben! Look out!" Sue called.

Ben and Reed spun and saw a nearby car bursting into flames as a spark hit its gas tank. Vehicles between them and the bridge exit began to explode in series.

Boom! Boom! Boom!

The blasts drew closer. Ben and Reed both knew they had only moments to live.

CHAPTER 9

BEN PUSHED REED ASIDE, trying to shield his friend from the explosions with his rocky body.

Sue suddenly became visible at Reed's side. A crowd of frightened people stood nearby, easily within blast range.

Reed stretched his arms to more than thirty feet wide, herding the crowd back. "Run!" he cried to them.

The car nearest to Ben exploded.

Sue screamed and threw up her arms reflexively to protect herself. Waves of a rippling transparent force field shot out from her hands, forming a bubble between the blast and her friends.

The explosion's fury crashed into Sue's invisible force field. The field buckled, but held back the roaring flames.

Sue staggered under the assault, trying to maintain her concentration. Sweat poured down her body. With all her mental strength, she flattened the force field toward the street, redirecting the blast back the way it came.

Unfortunately, the shock wave from the explosion deflected off the pavement and into a fire truck racing to the scene.

The fire truck careened sideways, brakes screaming. Its tail end slashed through the steel guardrail at the edge of the bridge.

The truck lurched backward, its rear dangling out over the river, hundreds of feet below. Firefighters manning the sides of the truck clung on for dear life as the crippled vehicle tottered on the edge.

Ben, protected from the blast by Sue's force field, ran forward and grabbed the front end of the truck. He caught hold just as it lurched toward the water. Ben dug in his heels, but the weight of the vehicle dragged him forward. His rocky feet scraped huge gouges in the road.

The firefighters screamed as their equipment fell into the water. They clawed their way back toward the bridge, hoping to make it before the truck fell, too.

Ben howled, straining with all his might to keep the fire truck on the bridge. His muscles bulged beneath his craggy orange skin.

He grunted in pain and took one step back, then another. Then another. Each step brought a new roar of agony, but Ben wouldn't give up.

With a mighty heave, he pulled the truck level and back onto the bridge. Firefighters scrambled off the truck, some of them even climbing over Ben's stony body.

Reed continued to help with the evacuation while Sue contained several more blasts with her invisible force field.

As the explosions stopped, she collapsed to the ground, her energy gone.

Ben pulled the truck back a few more feet, so it couldn't possibly fall, and then dropped to his knees, exhausted.

Several wary police officers drew closer and leveled their guns at the four exhausted superhumans.

But the rescued firefighters broke into applause, as did the crowd of rescued civilians standing nearby.

"They saved us all," one firefighter said.

Johnny and Sue's clothes had been badly damaged in the disaster. Two firefighters stepped forward and gave the pair their coats.

Reed and Ben exchanged tired glances.

"One minute we're monsters, the next, heroes," Ben said. "Go figure."

Reed shrugged.

Ben spotted someone familiar in the crowd: Debbie.

He stood and walked toward her. "Make way," he said. "Give a guy some room."

But by the time he reached the spot where his fiancée

had stood, she was gone. On the pavement lay a small glittering object: Debbie's engagement ring.

Ben reached down to pick up the ring, but it was too small for his huge fingers. He looked at it hopelessly.

Reed scooped it up for him.

"I swear to you," Reed said quietly, "I will do everything in my power until there is not one breath left in me. You are going to be Ben Grimm again." He pressed the ring into Ben's rocky hand.

Ben nodded, wanting to believe.

As dawn broke over New York, Victor sat in his office, watching a replay of the bridge disaster on a huge flat screen monitor.

"Amazingly," the newscaster said, "no one was killed in the accident."

Victor watched as the crowd of firefighters applauded Ben, Sue, Johnny, and Reed. The four looked tired, but heroic.

Victor's body stiffened as Reed protectively adjusted the firefighter's jacket around Sue's shoulders.

The businessman sat up straight in his chair, his hands clenching the armrests, hard. To his shock, the armrests shattered under his grip.

Victor looked down at his hands. Near the fingernails, his flesh looked almost *metallic*.

* * *

Johnny smiled. "I thought I was a goner when that blast hit, but the flames washed right over me," he said. "The force knocked me down, but other than that . . ."

He and the others paced the emergency holding tent where they'd been taken after the accident. Nearby, police, fire, and rescue were busy coordinating the cleanup of the accident scene.

"We were lucky," Reed responded. "We may have amazing powers, but we're not immortal."

"You sure?" Johnny asked, half-serious.

"Let's go," Ben said. "I'm tired of all this waiting around. Next thing you know, they'll want to put us in the circus."

Reed and Sue nodded, and all four of them turned to leave.

The fire chief poked his head into the tent. "There's some folks outside who want to see you," he said.

Reed shook his head. "We're not going public," he said. "We're scientists, not celebrities."

The chief smiled. "Try *superheroes*." He walked to the corner of the tent and turned on a small TV. Every network showed footage from the amazing rescue.

"They're calling you the *Fantastic Four*," the chief said.

"Cool," said Johnny. He headed for the exit.

"Johnny, slow down," Sue called.

He paused for a moment, then dashed outside.

Sue, Ben, and Reed swapped worried glances.

"No way that punk should be our spokesman," Ben said.

They all hurried out after Sue's younger brother.

Johnny reached the crowd ahead of the rest. Cameras whirred and flashed, digital video rolled. Johnny drank it all in.

Just behind, the others stopped, stunned by the sea of reporters. The mayor met them at the microphones. "Which one of you is the leader?" he asked.

"That'd be me," Johnny replied eagerly.

"No, seriously," the mayor said.

Ben and Sue instinctively turned to Reed. The mayor ushered him to the microphone.

Reed looked out over the assembled expectant faces and swallowed hard.

"Say something!" Sue whispered.

"Uh . . . ," Reed began. "During our recent mission to the Von Doom Space Station, we were exposed to an as-yet-unidentified cosmic energy, probably some kind of nucleotide compound . . ."

"What kind of *powers* do you have?" one reporter shouted. Clearly, no one in the crowd came for a science lecture. "Can any of you fly?"

"I'm working on it," Johnny put in.

"We don't know much more than you do, at this point," Sue said. "Which is why we're going directly to a lab, where we can diagnose our symptoms in order to . . ."

"Symptoms?" another reporter interjected. "I thought you had *powers*."

Reed and Sue exchanged an uneasy glance.

"We *do*," Johnny said. "We're going to blow your minds. There's a new day dawning—the day of the Fantastic Four."

"That *thing* there doesn't look so fantastic," someone shouted.

Ben balled his hands into fists, making a sound like rocks being crushed.

Reed stepped in front of Johnny, taking the microphone once more. "Ben Grimm is a genuine American hero," Reed said, "who's been through a terrible ordeal . . ."

Johnny jumped in again. "What he's trying to say is: Every team needs a mascot."

The reporters laughed. Cameras flashed, taking pictures of Ben. The "Thing" turned his head away from them.

"So," Johnny said, trying to take control once more, "first up on our superhero docket is . . ."

"Diagnosing this," Reed said, cutting him off. "And controlling it. That is our first and only priority right now."

The crowd seemed disappointed.

"Thank you," Reed concluded. "No more questions."

He, Sue, Ben, and even Johnny walked away. The crowd surged toward them, but Ben turned back and held up one massive finger.

"Be nice," he rumbled.

The press backed off.

Victor had nearly paced a hole in the carpet of the bank's waiting room. He did *not* look happy.

"Reed's comments at that press conference *killed* us," Leonard said. "Nobody wants to invest in a biotech company that turns its workers into circus freaks."

Victor scratched the bandage on his forehead. Every day, his scar grew larger.

Ned Cecil, the head banker, came out of a nearby meeting room to talk to Victor.

"Well, Victor," he said, "the bank would like to congratulate you—on the fastest business free fall we've seen since the Depression. We can't even *give* your stock away."

He motioned to a newspaper lying on a coffee table. Ben Grimm's transformed face stared back from the cover.

"You promised a cure-all and came back with *this*." He gestured toward a video monitor on the wall, playing a silent news feed of the bridge incident.

Victor's blood pressure rose. The image on the screen flickered slightly. He looked down at his hands, wondering.

"I've got a way to turn this around," he said.

"Which is?" Cecil asked.

"Simple," Victor replied. "I *cure* them. If I can cure these . . . freaks, then I can cure anyone. What better way to restore our reputation?"

Ned thought a moment. "One week," he said. "Or the bank pulls out, and you cover your losses."

Victor nodded grimly.

CHAPTER 10

THE DOORMAN stepped aside and held the door open as Reed, Sue, Johnny, and Ben entered the lobby of the Baxter Building.

"Welcome back to the Baxter, Dr. Richards," the doorman said. He motioned toward the crowd of reporters outside. "Is all that for you?"

"I'm afraid so, uh, . . ." Reed replied. He searched his mind for the man's name and couldn't come up with it.

"Jimmy," Sue said, stepping in. "Good to see you again."

Jimmy smiled at both of them. "Good to see you, too."

"Any visitors while I was away?" Reed asked.

"Just the usual," Jimmy replied. "And the mail." He opened a drawer full of envelopes in his desk by the door.

Reed glanced at them. They were all from banks; none looked friendly.

"We had a tough year," Reed explained to Sue and Johnny.

"Yeah," Ben said, "nine years straight."

The four of them stepped into the elevator and pressed the button for the twentieth floor, the bottom floor of Reed's top-floor complex.

The elevator didn't move. The readout on the digital panel declared: MAXIMUM WEIGHT CAPACITY EXCEEDED.

Ben sighed. "I'll take the stairs." He lumbered off to the stairway as the others rode up. An uneasy silence filled the elevator.

Finally, Johnny asked, "How come Ben can't turn it on and off like us?"

"He was exposed the longest," Reed explained. "So his DNA mutated faster. Our genes are still recombining."

Sue nodded, understanding. "That's why yesterday we were normal, today we're not, and tomorrow . . ."

"We'll be full-on twenty-four-seven fantastic?" Johnny asked enthusiastically.

"Grow up, Johnny," Sue said. "Do you want to run around on *fire* for the rest of your life?"

Johnny thought a moment. "Uh . . . yeah. Is that a trick question?"

"If I can understand this," Reed said, "I can control it."

"And if you can't," Sue said, "then it controls us." She looked worried.

They stepped out of the elevator into Reed's scientific laboratory complex. It wasn't quite as grand as Victor's tower, but it still took up more than twenty stories of the skyscraper's top floors. Much of the space remained open—a massive, skylit atrium, with room for Reed's larger experiments.

Reed led Sue and Johnny to the individual living apartments. Ben soon caught up with them.

"I think we should *all* stay here until we can define the extent of our changes," Reed said, "and figure out how to reverse them." He glanced guiltily at Ben.

Johnny flopped down on his bed. "You got cable?" he asked.

The Storms spent the next half hour unpacking and arranging their possessions in their new quarters. Just as Sue finished putting things away, someone knocked on the door.

She was surprised to see Victor standing in the doorway.

"I've been so worried about you," he said.

"Victor," Sue replied, "I'm sorry. I didn't get a chance . . ."

"Please," he said, "no apologies. I've arranged for your things to be moved to one of my condos. You'll have round-the-clock care." He reached for her bags.

"Thank you," she said. "That's generous. But I think I should stay here, with my brother, until we get a handle on this."

Victor looked startled at the rebuff. He managed a thin smile. "Of course you should," he agreed.

She nodded awkwardly as Reed came in. "Victor," he said. "What are you doing here?"

"Just checking on my friends," Victor replied. "How much do you know about your ailments?"

"Not much," said Reed. "We'll need to run tests to see the extent of the cellular damage."

Victor nodded. "Well, let me know if there is anything I can do. We're in this together."

He shook Reed's hand. His grip was so tight that Reed's elastic fingers compressed slightly. Victor shook Sue's hand as well. He smiled and quickly headed for the main exit.

Reed ran to catch up and speak with him.

"Victor, wait," he began. "I'm sorry the mission didn't go as planned."

Victor wheeled on him, eyes blazing with anger.

"Didn't go as *planned*?" Von Doom scoffed. "It was a *catastrophe*. You ruined the lives of four people!"

"If you think I could feel any worse . . . ," Reed said.

"I put my company, my name, billions of dollars on the line," Victor snapped. "I will *not* let you make me look like a fool."

"I don't know what happened," Reed said. "The storm wasn't supposed to be there for days."

"Well, for once in your life, you *didn't* have all the answers. And now we're *all* paying the price," Victor said.

Reed glanced up at the scar protruding from the large bandage on Victor's head. Victor put his hand to the scar. The lights in the corridor dimmed and flickered.

The billionaire glanced at them, annoyed. "Now pay your electric bill and get back to work." He stepped into the elevator, leaving Reed behind.

Before Victor had a chance to touch the button for the lobby, it lit up and the elevator began to move.

Victor slammed his fist into the elevator's steel wall. The wall buckled and dented.

He stepped back, shocked, and looked down at his knuckles. The skin had peeled away where his hand had struck the wall. Beneath he saw not flesh and blood, but a hard, metallic shell. The metal's dark surface pulsated with electrical energy.

He whispered quietly to himself, "What am I becoming? What has Richards done to me?"

Reed Richards, Ben Grimm, and Sue and Johnny Storm are about to go on a mission to space that will change their lives forever.

Up in space, Ben prepares to go on a space walk.

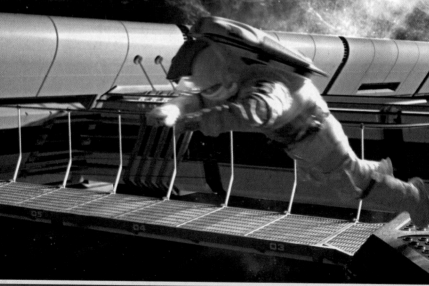

The mission doesn't go exactly as planned, when the cosmic storm comes early.

Reed and Johnny are powerless to help Ben.

Up in the control room, Victor Von Doom is only worried about saving himself.

The Thing tests his newfound strength . . .

Johnny, Reed, and Sue discover new powers of their own.

Ben uses the transformation chamber to turn back into the Thing.

Doctor Doom is ready for him.

The battle is on!

CHAPTER 11

REED FELT FRUSTRATED. The testing wasn't going well, especially with Ben. The scientific instruments had failed to penetrate the Thing's rocky skin.

"You got a chisel round here?" Ben asked wryly.

Reed was glad that his friend could joke about it, but if the tests couldn't identify the "disease" ravaging Ben's DNA, there was no way Reed—or anyone else—could possibly cure him.

Worry filled Reed's mind as he watched Ben easily hoist a six-ton weight over his head with one hand.

Johnny's powers proved just as impressive. In Reed's fireproof testing chamber, Johnny allowed his whole body to burst into flame.

The readouts on the temperature display shot up: 2,000 degrees Kelvin . . . 4,000 degrees . . . Johnny turned white-hot, became blinding to look at. The machines smoked as the readings climbed off the scale.

"Back it down, Johnny!" Reed said.

"I can go hotter," Johnny replied, not listening.

Reed pulled a switch on the wall and fire-retardant foam sprayed into the chamber, smothering Johnny's flames.

The hotshot pilot glared at Reed. "You're really crimping my style here," he said.

"You were approaching the temperature of a supernova," Reed explained.

"Excellent," Johnny said.

Sue, helping with the tests, said, "That's the temperature of an exploding sun. You could set fire to earth's atmosphere and destroy all life as we know it."

Johnny nodded reluctantly. "Gotcha. Supernova bad."

Reed looked forlornly at his melted and smoking equipment. He'd have to repair it before running more tests.

Besides scientific data, Reed needed more everyday information in order to diagnose his friends. He interviewed Ben and then moved on to Johnny.

"I'm trying to figure out why we each ended up with different symptoms," he explained.

"That's easy," Johnny shot back. "I'm hot. You're . . . well, let's face it, you're a bit of a limp noodle. Sue's always been easy to see through. And Ben's a beast." He glanced at Reed's pencil, hovering above the clipboard. "Why aren't you writing this down?"

Reed could tell it was going to be a long process. . . .

In order to monitor Sue's condition, he used advanced prismatic devices designed to measure light refraction.

"It's not *invisibility* per se," he explained to her. "You're bending the light around yourself with some kind of malleable force field."

She nodded, understanding. "That's what I projected on the bridge."

"Can you remember your exact emotional state when you did it?" Reed asked. "If we can locate the trigger . . ."

"Anger. Rage. Frustration," she replied.

"Okay," Reed said. "Is there any way to duplicate that feeling—some memory, or . . ."

She looked at Reed and her eyes narrowed.

Sue faded from view—although he could still "see" her on his advanced machinery. A baseball-sized bubble of force appeared, floating in front of her invisible face.

Reed stepped from behind the machinery. "How are you doing that . . . ," he began. The clear bubble shot at him like a bullet. Reed dodged, stretching his body out of the way like a rubber band. The force bubble smashed into the equipment behind him.

"I'm sorry," Sue said, returning to visibility once more. "I didn't mean to do that. You must think I'm still angry about our breakup."

"Why would I think that?" Reed asked. "I mean, *you* broke up with *me*."

"Are you kidding?" she replied.

"No," Reed said. "I distinctly remember . . . I came home, you were gone . . ."

Sue scowled. "You were waiting for me to walk out the door from the moment we met. You never believed in yourself—never believed in *us*."

Reed looked away. Sue's anger faded. She stepped closer to him.

"You know," she said, "I never thought I could feel more alone than the day my parents died. But, sometimes, I felt loneliest when I was with you."

Reed turned to her. "I'm sorry," he said. He picked up his clipboard. "Are there any negative side effects when you disappear?" he asked.

"You mean, aside from being *gone*?" she replied.

Before Reed could answer, Johnny marched into the lab. All that remained of his clothing was a few burned and tattered threads. "Okay, guys," he said, "we have a serious problem. I'm all for being superheroes, but there's no way I can go out in public if my clothes burn off every time I use my powers."

Reed sighed and went to run more tests.

A short time later, he assembled the others. "I've discovered that because our uniforms were exposed to the radiation, too, they now possess unstable molecules identical to our own. They will react adaptively to our transformations, becoming invisible, changing size on demand, or remaining impervious to flame."

By that afternoon, Reed, Sue, and Johnny had all changed into the blue formfitting uniforms.

"You look like an eighties rock band," Ben pointed out, as they checked themselves out in the mirror.

"Ben's right," Johnny said. "These costumes are missing something. I can't put my finger on it."

"They're not costumes," Reed said. "They're *uniforms.*"

"Johnny," Sue said, sensing trouble, "we've talked about this: Nobody leaves the lab until we've stabilized."

Johnny nodded and rolled his eyes. "Right, 'Mom.' Got it. I'm *grounded.*"

"So," Victor said to his doctor, "what's the prognosis?"

The two of them stared at an X-ray of Victor's arm. The metallic transformation seemed to be spreading.

"Your tissues, your organs, your entire biophysical structure is changing," the doctor replied. "Every system is still functioning, somehow, but . . ."

"And they're changing into . . . what?" Victor asked.

"I don't really know," the doctor said. "A compound organic-metallic alloy. Stronger than titanium, harder than diamonds."

"Like the shields Reed installed on my station," Victor mused. "Reed's shields." His eyes burned with cold fury. "How long?"

The doctor sighed. "At this rate, the infection should be complete in two, maybe three weeks. I'll notify the CDC and . . ."

"What?" Victor said angrily.

"The Centers for Disease Control," the doctor explained. "If this thing is contagious . . ."

Victor grabbed him by the throat.

"Look at me," the billionaire said. "I have a life, a woman I love. I'm the face of a multinational company. We need to keep this confidential, understand?"

"But this disease," the doctor countered, barely able to breathe, "is progressive, degenerative. You won't . . . survive."

"That's terrible news," Victor said.

With one cobra-swift move, he smashed his other hand into the doctor's chest, killing him instantly. Victor let the body fall. He looked at his hand, surprised by his own strength.

A cold smile drew over his face. "I think I'll get a second opinion."

CHAPTER 12

REED SLAMMED HIS HEAD down on his desk. All the tests he'd done on Ben had turned up nothing useful—no clue as to a cure.

"Nothing!" he muttered to himself.

He looked up. The desk had flattened his pliable face into mush, but it quickly regained its usual shape. He straightened out his papers, accidentally knocking a clear container off the desk.

Reed stretched his hand down and snatched the object up. It was one of the plant samples from the trip. He looked at it, an idea forming in his mind.

Less than an hour later, he had six chalkboards filled with equations, calculations, and notes. He stretched from one to the next, working on all of them simultaneously and inputting the results into a nearby computer. His rubbery limbs wound all over the room.

Sue entered the lab. "What are you doing?" she asked, thinking the rubber might have gotten to his head.

"I'm re-creating the cosmic storm, using the irradiated plant samples as a model for its composure," he replied. "Last time, I failed to account for the unstable molecules. This time . . ."

She slid up next to him to check his work. Reed looked uncomfortable.

"Would it be easier if I went invisible?" she asked.

"I'm just not used to sharing a lab," he replied.

Sue looked at the computer simulation. It showed an eerily accurate rendering of the cosmic storm. "Last time we saw *that*, things didn't work out so well," she noted.

"I won't make another mistake," Reed said. "I can't."

She sat down next to him and they began to work, side by side.

Victor watched the two of them on the surveillance screen in his office. He had paid through the teeth to set up the spy equipment in Reed's lab, but it had paid off, many times over. Victor scowled and toyed with the diamond ring he had intended to give Sue.

Leonard entered the room.

"Is Reed any closer to a cure?" he asked.

"The only thing he's closer to is Sue," Victor replied.

Leonard straightened his tie. "Three days, sir," he said. "Three days 'til the bank pulls out."

Victor nodded and leaned closer to the monitors. Static began to consume the picture. The flickering light reflected off Victor's peeling skin, revealing the metal beneath.

In his room at the Baxter Building, Ben watched an old videotape of his birthday. The tape was made less than a year ago, when he and Debbie were happy, in love, with the whole future ahead of them.

"What did you wish for, honey?" Debbie asked, as the old Ben blew out the candles on his cake.

"I already got it," he replied. "I got everything I want."

A tear trickled down the Thing's rocky cheek. He got up and went to check on Reed's progress.

The simulation of the cosmic storm on Reed's screen swirled faster. Reed wearily took notes.

"Reed, you've been here twenty-six hours straight," Sue said. "Go to sleep."

"I'll rest when I'm done," he replied.

"Newton discovered gravity while napping," Sue noted. "Einstein found the theory of relativity in a dream. You need to rest, before you're stretched too thin to think."

She wheeled her chair over next to him. Their eyes met

and locked. Both seemed about to say something, but they turned away and went back to work.

Ben watched the two of them, unseen, from the doorway.

He turned and left the building, wearing his trench coat disguise once more.

He went to his favorite bar, back in the old neighborhood.

Inside, music blared, lights flashed, people danced, drank, and enjoyed the Brooklyn nightlife. Ben pulled his hat low across his craggy forehead and squeezed through the door.

A big picture of Ben—the old Ben, from his astronaut heyday—hung in a prominent place over the bar. As the Thing entered, everyone in the room went silent.

Ben lumbered to the bar. People paid their bills and left, talking about him in hushed whispers on their way out. Ben ignored them.

"Good to be back home," he said. "Hey, Ernie. Sorry for killing your business. I'll take the usual."

The bartender went to fetch his drink. Ben looked around. Only one person remained in the place. A beautiful young woman with curly, dark brown hair sat at the other end of the bar.

Ben turned to her and said, "Why you still here? Didn't my looks scare you off?"

"You look okay to me, mister," she replied, staring at him with blank eyes.

Ben noticed her white cane. She was blind.

He shook his head. "Somebody up there hates me," he muttered. "Sorry about the crack."

"It sounds like you hate yourself," the woman replied.

"If you could see me, you'd hate me, too," Ben replied.

She took her cane and walked over to him. "Could I . . . see you?" she asked.

Ben didn't know what to say.

She touched his arm. "It's okay," she said, "I won't bite." She ran her fingers across the rocky skin. "Not that biting would do much good." She smiled. Her fingers crept up his arm until she found his face. She touched it gently, probingly.

"Such a sad face," she said. "You know, sometimes being different isn't a bad thing."

"Trust me," Ben said, "this ain't one of those times."

She took her cane, stood, and headed for the door. "See you around," she said. "I'm Alicia, by the way. Alicia Masters."

"Ben," he rumbled. "Ben Grimm."

"I know," she called back as she disappeared into the night.

Lights twinkled overhead in the fancy eatery as Sue joined Victor at his table. He stood and pulled out her chair with gloved hands.

"Thank you for coming out to see me," he said.

She nodded self-consciously. "Yes, well, I wanted to talk to you about Reed."

Victor smiled but, under the table, clenched his fist.

"Sue," he said in a measured, level voice, "I think maybe we should talk about *us*. You know, I was going to ask you something before all this happened."

Sue became slightly transparent.

"Look, Victor," she said, "I want you to know I appreciate everything you've done for me and I think you're a good man."

Victor gripped the table so hard, the dish settings atop it trembled. "Please, Sue," he said. "Don't humiliate me. Leave that to Reed." He took a deep breath. "I really hope you two are happy together."

"That's not what I wanted to talk about," she said. "There's nothing going on between me and . . ."

He interrupted her again. "Of course not. But he must *like* having his prize specimen under glass. Maybe that's why he hasn't found a cure yet."

Sue bristled; Victor leaned closer.

"It's ironic, isn't it?" he said. "You're finally the perfect woman for him—because you're *invisible*."

He rose so quickly and forcefully that the water glasses on the table splashed over. All eyes in the restaurant turned toward him as he stalked out.

As Victor left, he slipped the engagement ring out of his pocket and crushed it. The diamond dust trickled out from between his fingers.

At the table, Sue slowly disappeared.

A businessman seated nearby laughed. "I wish my wife would do that!" he said.

An invisible shove spilled wine across his shirt. The doors of the eatery swung open as Sue ran out, grateful that no one could see her.

CHAPTER 13

MEANWHILE, Ben and Sue weren't the only ones who had left the building. Johnny skidded a souped-up motorcycle out onto the dirt racetrack at the NYC Arena.

The announcer's voice boomed over the crowded grandstand. "Introducing our special guest, Johnny Storm of the Fantastic Four!"

Johnny zoomed the bike up the first hill and launched himself high into the air.

He arced up toward the domed ceiling, higher than any bike was made to go. As he did, flames began trailing from his back. The crowd gasped.

"Unbelievable, ladies and gentlemen!" the announcer crowed.

Johnny soared higher, acrobatically twisting the motorbike as he went. Higher and higher.

"That's gotta be a world record!" the announcer said.

Johnny pulled the handlebars back, trying to do a complete flip, but he lost hold. The bike slipped out of his hands and fell to the ground. Johnny's momentum carried him the opposite way, right toward the startled crowd.

He waved his arms, trying desperately to change direction. As he did, his entire body burst into flame. He zoomed over the crowd, a trail of hot wind trailing in his wake. Dust from the track billowed up in huge clouds.

I'm flying! he thought.

As soon as he started thinking about it, though, he lost concentration and plummeted to the ground. He crashed hard into one of the hay bales placed as crash bumpers around the track.

The crowd gasped and then fell silent. Johnny looked around. Nothing seemed broken. He sprang to his feet.

The grandstand crowd rose and gave him a standing ovation.

Johnny waved and blew kisses to his adoring fans. He made his way to the trackside TV announcer.

"Nice costume," the announcer said.

"Thanks," Johnny replied. A big white "4" logo on the front of his uniform shone brightly in the arena's spotlights.

Back in the Baxter Building, Ben stomped angrily around the recreation room.

Reed and Sue rushed in. "Ben!" Reed said. "What's going on?"

Ben stabbed one big finger toward Johnny's smiling face on the TV.

Reed's mouth dropped almost to the floor.

"He didn't," Reed said.

"Oh, he did," Ben replied.

"So," the reporter asked Johnny, "what are your super-hero names?"

"You can call me the Human Torch," Johnny replied. "The ladies call me Torch."

"What about the rest of the team?"

It seemed as though Johnny hadn't given much thought to this. "Uh," he said, "we call my sister the . . . Invisible Girl."

"Girl?!" Sue blurted.

"What about your leader, Dr. Reed Richards?" the announcer pressed.

"I wouldn't exactly say he's the leader," Johnny said, "but we call him . . . Mr. Fantastic."

Reed sighed.

The reporter held up a picture of Ben, postaccident. "And what about this one, Agent Orange? What do you call this thing?"

Johnny smiled right at the camera. "That's it. Just the

Thing. We would have gone with Rocky Road, but there were rights issues."

The TV audience laughed.

Ben didn't. "Okay, I'm gonna go kill him now."

He turned and left. Sue and Reed glanced at each other and followed.

"I'm driving," Sue said.

A short time later, Johnny strode out of the NYC Arena. His red sports car waited for him, parked out front.

He stopped on his way to the car to sign autographs and chat with fans. He didn't notice Sue and Reed heading his way, glaring at him like angry parents.

Johnny reached the parking area and looked around. "Where's my ride?" he asked.

As he spoke, a skidding sound caught his attention. He turned and saw a mass of metal, four feet square, sliding down the street toward him. Red paint and chrome poked out through the wreckage.

"My car!" he gasped.

The car's license plate sailed through the air, hit him in the head, and rattled to the ground. The Thing dusted off his stony hands and smiled.

"You're gonna pay for that, rock-head!" Johnny said.

"So," Sue interjected, "the Human Torch is now the official face of the Fantastic Four?"

Ben balled his fists as he marched toward Johnny. "He's about to be a *broken* face."

"Johnny," Reed said, "we need to stay out of sight until we're normal again."

"What if some of us don't *want* to be 'normal' again?" Johnny countered. "We didn't *all* turn into monsters, like . . ."

The Thing reeled back his fist. The Human Torch flinched, but Ben merely turned and walked away.

Johnny hurled a fireball at him. It smacked into the back of Ben's head. Ben whirled, more shocked than hurt.

"Did you just . . . ?" he began.

Johnny hit him with another fireball, this time in the face.

"Okay," Ben bellowed, "that's it, Tinkerbell!"

He charged, ready to smash Johnny to pieces.

Reed stepped in between. Ben couldn't stop. His fist smashed into Mr. Fantastic's chest, stretching it like rubber.

Reed's pliable body bent back, smashing into Johnny. Johnny flew off his feet and slammed into the hood of a parked car.

"You wanted to fly?" Ben said. "Fly!"

Johnny sat up. The paint bubbled where his hands touched the hood. He stood, his fists blazing balls of fire.

"Let's see if we can get blood from a stone," he snarled.

He and Ben locked eyes and sprinted toward each other, quickly covering the half block between them. Ben's feet cracked the sidewalk as he ran; his footsteps sounded like thunder. Waves of heat rolled off Johnny's body.

Just before they crashed together, Sue stepped between them. She froze both men with a stare. "You two need a time out," she said.

"Blockhead started it," Johnny complained.

Ben turned and stalked away through the crowd that had gathered to watch the fight. A paparazzi photographer appeared and snapped pictures. Ben grabbed his camera, crushed it, and kept going.

Sue glared at Johnny, then ran after Ben. She waded through the throng of curious New Yorkers, trying to catch up with her friend. "Ben, slow down!" she cried.

"Oh my gosh!" a teenage girl screamed. "That's him! The Thing!"

The girl darted out into the street, oblivious to the oncoming cars. A taxicab headed straight toward her.

Instinctively, Sue reached out with her powers and used an invisible force field to push the girl out of the way. The taxicab whizzed by harmlessly. The girl stood, stunned, by the side of the road. People crowded around to see if she was okay.

Sue and Ben kept walking.

"Johnny didn't mean it," Sue said. "You know him. He's always been a hothead."

"It's not him," Ben said, "it's *them*." He pointed at the crowd. "I can't live like this. You don't know what it's like to . . ."

She cut him off. "Have people stare? Whisper?"

Ben shook his head. "You got no idea what I'd give to be invisible. Your nightmare is my *dream*."

Sue didn't know what to say.

Ben walked off into the gathering dusk.

"You've got to learn to hold back," Reed told Johnny.

"See, that's your problem," Johnny replied. "You *always* want to hold back. What if we've got these gifts for a *reason*? What if we have some, you know, like, calling?"

"A higher calling like getting girls and making money," Reed replied.

Johnny missed the sarcasm. "Is there any higher?" he asked.

He stepped into the sea of fans surrounding them, shaking hands, and signing autographs.

Reed stood alone on the steps of the arena, looking at the wreckage they'd caused: the cracked sidewalk, the melted car hood, the compacted sports car.

Would every day of their lives be like this?

CHAPTER 14

VICTOR STOOD in the boardroom of banker Ned Cecil. Both of them stared at a TV, showing the events in front of the NYC Arena.

"They don't look too cured to me," the banker said. Other bankers sat in the room with him, staring coldly at Victor.

Victor rubbed the large bandage on his forehead. "Maybe we can use this publicity to . . ."

Ned cut him off. "Victor, stop. The bank's lost enough already. This isn't a negotiation, it's a *notification*. We're pulling out."

The other bankers got up and filed out of the room.

Victor boiled inside. Sparks of electricity danced within the gloves hiding his hands.

"I'm sorry," Ned said. He left, too.

The lights in the room dimmed, then sparked and burst.

Victor leaped into action.

He caught up with the banker in the shadows of the underground parking lot.

"Hello?" Ned called nervously. "Who's there?" At first, he didn't see Victor in the darkness. The banker held on to his car's open door as though it were a security blanket. Victor stepped from the shadows.

Ned sighed with relief. "Mr. Von Doom," he said. "No hard feelings, right? It's nothing personal, just dollars and cents."

Victor said nothing.

"Consider this a valuable lesson," Ned continued. "Everyone has to learn their place, Vic, even you." When Victor still didn't reply, he added, "Hey, it could be worse. You could be one of those Fantastic Freaks."

Electricity crackled around Victor's body. His eyes narrowed. He slammed his palm down on the hood of the banker's car. A deadly charge of electricity coursed through the vehicle into Ned, who was still holding the door.

The banker slumped over the front seat, dead.

"Fantastic Four," Victor said, seething. "There were *five*."

He returned to his office. The lights sprang on as he looked toward the switch.

His surveillance monitors also flickered to life as he approached. He located Reed in one of the labs at the Baxter Building. Victor's eyes narrowed.

Leonard entered the room. "Did you hear what happened at the bank?" he asked, upset.

"Yes," Victor replied. "Tragic."

"Sir, are you okay?" Leonard asked.

"Never better, Leonard. Never stronger. But I think it's time for us to accelerate Reed's *process*."

"How?" Leonard asked.

"With the right kind of pressure," Victor replied. "Everything has its breaking point. We'll see just how far Dr. Richards can bend."

He picked up a newspaper from the coffee table and pointed to a picture of the Thing on the front. "Locate our lab rat," he said. "And I'll go see the good doctor."

Reed wrapped his pliable arms around a huge stack of boxes and carried them into a room he'd dubbed the "transformation lab." The boxes were taller and wider than any normal man could have carried, but they were no problem for the elastic arms of Mr. Fantastic.

As he set the boxes down, he saw Victor standing by the computer, reading his experiment notes.

"The shields," Victor said quietly. "Of course. You're building a chamber with the station shields."

"They're the only thing that can withstand the energy from the cosmic particles," Reed explained.

Victor nodded. "So, you'll re-create the storm in miniature in the chamber. Then you'll heat it up, and reverse the . . ."

"Polarity, right," Reed said, finishing the thought. "Extract the radiation and reverse the DNA mutation."

Victor gazed at Reed's half-complete machine, marveling. "How long 'til it's ready?" he asked. As he stepped toward the simulation screen, the tiny storm inside swirled faster.

"Three, four weeks," Reed replied. "I need to make sure the storm's stable, or it could make us worse."

"Then *we'll* build the machine while you check the specs," Victor said. "Reed, we've *got* to do this. Think about Ben. If it saves just one day, that could be the day that saves his life."

Reed looked at his machine and then at the computer simulation.

Slowly, he nodded.

An army of Von Doom technicians filled the Baxter Building. They worked according to Reed's plans and Victor's instructions. The shield walls for the transformation chamber began to slowly rise.

Sue entered the room, surprised at the activity. A worried look crossed her face as she joined Reed and Victor.

"I thought we weren't ready to . . . ," she began.

"You weren't," Victor replied. "You just needed a little help. Well, I'll leave you experts to it." He smiled at her and walked away.

Sue stepped closer to Reed. "Don't let Victor push you to get what he wants," she said. "We're not ready, and you know it."

He looked torn. "I know that, but . . . ," he said. He twisted his rubbery neck and glanced at Victor over his shoulder. "Victor can be very persuasive."

He took a deep breath. "My mind's whirling. I could use a break to clear my head. Care to join me?"

Sue nodded. "A break would do us both good," she said.

The Thing lumbered down the streets of Brooklyn, staying in the evening shadows, keeping to himself.

People stopped, stared, and pointed as he stomped past. Ben ignored them.

He was so wrapped up in his own thoughts that he almost didn't see the sculpture in the window of a small art gallery. He stopped, backed up, and looked again. Sure enough, it was a bust of *his* head and shoulders.

Ben stared at the exquisitely sculpted version of his own stony face.

"I figured the only way to get you here was to stick that in the window," a familiar voice said.

Alicia stood in the gallery's doorway.

"How'd you know it was me?" he asked.

"I'm blind, not deaf," she replied. "Wanna come in?"

Ben glanced through the doorway into the gallery behind her. There was a party going on. "I'm really not dressed for a shindig," he told her.

"Relax," she said. "It's casual."

"No," Ben said, "I mean I'm a little . . . dusty."

Alicia smiled and led him into her studio. There, she used a pressure hose to wash him down and small carving tools to clean out the crevices in his stony armor.

"I was wondering when you'd walk by," she said as she worked. Her touch was gentle, kind.

"You could've put an ad in the personals," he replied.

"Sensual blind chick seeks three-ton he-man for deep spiritual relationship?" she suggested.

"This ain't permanent," Ben said. "My friend Reed's working on a cure. Anyway, he was . . ."

"You're fine with me just as you are," she said, smiling.

It was only dusk, but stars already shone brightly overhead at the Hayden Planetarium. The voice of the lecturing astronomer droned in the darkness.

The man sitting in the last row let his disguised features slip back to normal and became Reed once more. Sue faded to visibility in the seat beside him. With the Fantastic Four's sudden fame, this was the only way they could get into the planetarium unnoticed.

They slumped down in their seats, like teenagers, and gazed up at the projected stars. "Remember our first date here?" Reed asked.

Sue nodded. Her face looked nostalgic and a little sad. "I remember our *last*," she replied. "I waited three hours—tried to count all the stars."

Reed looked at her apologetically. "Sue," he said, "there's something I need to tell you—something I lied about." He took a deep breath. "I *did* notice when you left. I noticed the moment you walked out the door. I let you go because I thought it was what you wanted."

She looked confused.

"You always said you wanted a stronger man," he explained, "more confident, courageous."

"I did, Reed," she replied. "But I wanted *you* to be that man. I left hoping you'd come after me—hoping you'd fight to keep me."

"What?" Reed asked, surprised. "Why didn't you tell me?"

"That would have kinda defeated the purpose," she said. "But, Reed . . . I'm telling you now."

"I'm not that man anymore," Reed said. "I'm tired of

coming in second and pushing away the people who mean the most to me."

He took her hand and she faded slightly. He looked earnestly at her.

"Just when you're starting to see me," she whispered, "there's less and less to see."

"I can see you fine," he said.

"Then prove it," she replied.

She disappeared entirely, but Reed leaned in to kiss her anyway.

"That's my nose, genius," she said. "These are my lips."

This time, Dr. Richards got it right.

Ben and Alicia joined the party at the Kirby Gallery. As they entered, all eyes turned to the orange, rocky-skinned Thing.

Ben looked around nervously. A whisper ran through the crowd. But it passed quickly and people were soon back to chatting as if nothing had happened.

Alicia smiled. "Look around," she suggested. "I'll get us drinks. They always let blind girls cut the line."

He watched her walk into the crowd. Despite her handicap, she was graceful and confident and—judging from the sculpture—one heck of an artist.

Ben hung back near the wall. Several patrons walked past, mistaking him for one of the exhibit's statues.

"I don't know about this one," a woman with a half-empty wineglass said as she stared at Ben. "It lacks a certain . . . realism."

"Alicia's always had a thing for runaways and strays," her companion replied, "but this is ridiculous."

"I know," the first woman agreed. "Did she really think these sculptures would sell?"

"Like anybody would want this *thing* in their home."

The first woman shook her head. "That girl's a one-woman charity."

Ben stood frozen, devastated by their words. He looked around at all the people talking and laughing. Were they laughing at him? Alicia giggled as she spoke to someone at the bar, too.

He was just a joke to all of them.

Ben turned and stomped out into the night.

CHAPTER 15

BEN SAT AT THE COUNTER of the diner and sipped coffee from a metal bowl. None of the other patrons sat within four chairs of him.

"Is this seat taken?" a familiar voice asked.

Ben turned as Victor spoke. He looked less dapper than usual. A large bandage covered most of his forehead.

"What are *you* doing here?" Ben asked.

"I'm worried about you," Victor replied.

"About me?" Ben said. "How sweet."

"Let me buy you some breakfast," Victor offered. "It looks like you could use the company."

Ben thought a moment, then nodded.

They took a window booth. Victor sipped coffee while the Thing finished his fourth foot-high stack of pancakes.

"I know what it's like to lose something you love,"

Victor told him. "To see it slip away and know it's never coming back."

"Reed's gonna fix me up," Ben said.

"I hope you're right," Victor replied. "I'm sorry if that sounds skeptical."

"Skeptical?" the Thing asked.

Victor leaned forward. "Well, if Reed hadn't made that mistake in the first place . . . Look, he's a brilliant man. We should trust he's working as hard as he can. You're his best friend. So what possible reason could he have for taking so much time?"

Ben wondered. Was there a grain of truth in what Victor said?

Reed and Sue returned to the Baxter Building. They laughed quietly, happy together for the first time in a long time. They flicked on the lights. Ben stood, statuelike, before them. They stopped laughing.

"Yeah," Ben said. "I have that effect on people."

"Ben . . . ," Reed began. He glanced from his friend to the transformation chamber, which had been completed while he and Sue were out.

"Oh," Ben said, "you remember my name, do you? You happen to remember what you *swore* to do with every breath in your body?" He stepped closer, menacingly.

"We're working as hard as we can," Reed said.

"I can tell," Ben said sarcastically. "Victor was right."

"Ben, don't," Sue said.

"This is between me and Reed," he replied.

"Ben," Reed said, "I don't know if this chamber will change us back or make us worse. Be patient a bit longer, while we run some tests."

"I'm *done* being patient!" Ben snapped. He poked one stony finger into Reed's chest and shoved him.

Reed stumbled, but Ben grabbed his face, pinching hard enough to distort Reed's rubbery features. "Look at me, Reed," Ben raged. "*You* did this! You destroyed my life!"

He thrust the scientist backward, and Reed toppled to the floor.

"That's why I can't make the same mistake twice," Reed explained desperately. "Don't you understand? I can't let it happen again. I've got to get it right, and it's *not* right yet! We need to test this!"

Ben looked down at Reed. The Thing's anger melted into sadness and betrayal.

"I spent my whole life protecting you," Ben said, "all the way from the schoolyard to the stars. For what? So you could play Twister with your girlfriend while I'm the freak of the week?"

Reed tried to stand, but Ben knocked him back down.

"Good thing you're flexible enough to watch your own back," Ben concluded, "'cause I won't be. Not anymore. You're on your own now." He turned and stomped out.

Sue wiped a trickle of blood from Reed's forehead.

"I'm okay," Reed said. "Just go after him. Stop him."

After she'd left, Reed stood and looked at the transformation machine—complete, but not ready. He came to a decision.

He switched the machine on.

Watching on the surveillance monitors in his office a mile away, Victor smiled.

Sue ran down the hallway, trying to catch up to Ben. But he beat her to the freight elevator and pressed the DOWN button.

Rushing to leave the lobby, he nearly bowled over Johnny.

"Check it out!" Johnny said. "Christmas come early!" He thrust an orange, rocky action figure into Ben's face. It was a bloated, even uglier version of the Thing. Johnny pressed a button on the Thing's back.

"It's clobberin' time!" the toy bellowed.

With one hand Ben grabbed Johnny and pushed him up against the wall. With the other, he snatched the toy away and smashed it into the wall beside the youngster's head.

"C-c-clobberin' time!" the toy repeated.

"Hey!" Johnny said. "That's a prototype!"

"Yeah?" Ben snarled. "Well, now it's *art*."

He dropped Johnny and stomped out the door.

When Sue reached the ground floor, she found her brother collecting his luggage from the doorman.

"Johnny," she said, "what's going on?"

"I called in and had Jimmy pack my stuff," he replied. "I'm moving out, back to the real world."

She pointed at his flashy uniform. "Is that what you call 'real'?" she asked.

He bristled. "At least it beats living in a cage like somebody's science project. Look around, sis! Stop talking to me like I'm your little boy."

"I will," she said, "as soon as you stop *acting* like one. You think those people out there care about you? They're not your family. They're not even your friends. You're just a *fad* to them."

He grabbed his bags and stepped toward the door. "Let's try something new: You live your life, and I'll live mine. And just for the record, they *love* me."

"Fine," she said. "Go. But if you're gonna run around calling yourself 'fantastic,' try and live up to it."

He turned and walked off into the night.

Sue tried hard to keep her composure. Even though they'd just begun, the Fantastic Four was already finished.

CHAPTER 16

THE TRANSFORMATION CHAMBER'S high-pitched whine filled Reed's laboratory. Reed hesitated in front of the booth, uncertain.

Across town, Victor watched on his spy cameras.

Behind Victor, swarms of workers brought crates into his private conference room—raw materials for his new project. Victor paid no attention to them as he focused on Reed.

Dr. Richards stepped into the chamber. He glanced up at the controlled power of the cosmic storm roiling above his head.

He took a deep breath and spread his arms wide, welcoming whatever might come, as the activation sequence counted down. The storm grew larger, enveloping him.

Reed's body jerked, as though he'd been struck by lightning. He twisted and distorted, vibrated out of control. He screamed.

The screens in Victor's office went black. He rose and looked out the window, gazing at the Baxter Building, a mile away. The top of the skyscraper glowed with power as the rest of its lights dimmed, and then went out.

Victor smiled.

When the emergency lights in the Baxter Building flickered on, Sue immediately sensed what had happened.

She ran upstairs, threw open the lab door, and raced inside.

Reed lay on the floor, barely conscious. His body was stretched and distorted. He looked like a human pile of spaghetti. His experiment was inconclusive. The chamber didn't work.

Sue kneeled at his side and supported his rubbery head. "What did you do, Reed?" she gasped. "What did you do?"

She struggled, trying to lift him, but it was as though he had no bones at all. One side of his face seemed to be melted. He gazed pathetically up at her. "Oh, Reed!" she said.

Victor barged into the lab. He stopped in the shadows by the doorway and gazed at Reed, in Sue's arms.

"It didn't work," he said, disappointed.

"I can . . . make it work," Reed mumbled. As he spoke, his body began to re-form slowly.

"Reed, stop," Sue said. "You need to rest."

"What makes you think it can work?" Victor asked. He took a step closer, but remained in the shadows.

"The power," Reed gasped. "We need . . . more energy to control . . . the storm."

"Let me see your data," Victor said.

"Victor!" Sue snapped. "He's hurt! This machine nearly killed him. We need to get him to a doctor."

Reed tried to say something more, but passed out instead. Victor looked at the machine, still humming, still drawing power from the rest of the building.

"You're right," he said. "Let's get Reed out of here."

He helped Sue carry the injured scientist back to his own room. They laid Reed on the bed. Sue kneeled at his side, tending to him.

Victor backed out into the hallway. He pulled out his cell phone and said, "Bring me our lab rat."

Ben sat alone under the Brooklyn Bridge, gazing at the city lights, thinking about cruel fate.

As he pondered, a limo screeched to a stop nearby. The limo door opened, and Leonard got out. "Ben," Von Doom's henchman said, "they need you back at the Baxter Building. It's Reed."

Ben considered his options a moment, then climbed into the car.

Colorful streaks of flame zipped around the ceiling at a swank Manhattan nightclub. Johnny sat in the VIP balcony, controlling the "light show." Throngs of admiring young women surrounded him, climbing all over one another to watch the Human Torch's tricks.

Johnny leaned close to one of the pretty girls and whispered, "What do you say we get out of here?"

The girl glanced from Johnny to the very large man standing behind her.

"This your boyfriend?" Johnny asked.

The man didn't look too happy. "Is that all you do?" he asked. "Bar tricks and stealing chicks?"

Johnny tapped the man's drink, and it burst into flame. The man dropped it. It smashed to the floor, spreading the fire. He quickly stamped it out.

"What are you doing?" the girl asked Johnny angrily. "You could have burned somebody!" She took her boyfriend's hand and headed for the door. Just before leaving, she called back, "You know, if I had your power, I'd be doing something *real* with it—not wasting my time doing cheap tricks in bars to impress some other guy's girl."

Johnny's face reddened. He looked around for support, but no one would meet his eye. Gradually the crowd shrunk back, leaving him alone in the middle of the noisy bar.

Sue had been right. These people didn't really like him. They weren't his friends, and they certainly weren't *family*.

Leonard led the Thing into Reed's lab. The transformation chamber sat open in the middle of the room. Victor stood by the control station.

"Ben, come in," he said.

"What is this?" Ben asked. "Where's Reed?"

"Where do you think? With Sue."

Ben glanced up at the lights in the room, which flickered oddly. "What do you want, Vic?" he asked.

"To help you," Victor replied. "I've run every test known to man, and they all yield the same result: The machine is *ready*."

Ben shook his head. "Reed said it'd be days, weeks, 'til . . ."

"He also said that we'd avoid the storm in space," Victor reminded him, "and we all know how that turned out."

Ben nodded and moved closer to the machine.

"Reed couldn't generate enough power for the machine to reach critical mass," Victor continued. "Yet another mistake for 'Mr. Fantastic.'"

"And *you* can power it up?" Ben asked.

"Yes," Von Doom said. "I've found a new energy source." The flickering lights kept him in the darkness. Behind his back, where Ben couldn't see, sparks sizzled on his fingertips. "Tell me, what would you do to be Ben Grimm again?"

Ben looked at the machine. He took a deep breath. "Let's do it."

CHAPTER 17

THE THING stepped into the transformation chamber. Victor pressed a button and the doors slowly slid closed, trapping Ben inside.

Von Doom manipulated the machine's controls, initiating the transformation sequence. The re-created cosmic storm swirled faster as energy poured into the chamber. The lights in the room flickered and went out, but still there wasn't enough power.

Victor walked over to the power generator. He grabbed it with both hands and concentrated. Energy surged out of his body, flowing into the machine. On the control panel, the transformation countdown began: 5 . . . 4 . . . 3 . . . 2 . . . 1 . . .

The Thing screamed as the energy of the cosmic storm, augmented by Von Doom's power, coursed through his body.

Across the city, lights flickered as power was drawn through Victor and into the Baxter Building. The top of the skyscraper lit up like a flare.

At the front door of the building, Johnny looked up and wondered what was happening. Inside, Sue gasped as the lights flickered once more. Reed, still injured, moaned.

The transformation chamber rattled dangerously as the power surged. The building shook right down to its foundations. The cosmic cloud swirled and sparked with energy.

Then, suddenly, it all stopped.

The lights within the chamber died, and the door slid open.

Ben stepped out and collapsed.

He wasn't the Thing anymore, but a normal man.

"It—it worked." He gasped. "Thank you. Thank you, Victor."

Victor didn't reply.

"Vic?" Ben asked. Victor was no longer manning the controls. Ben looked around and spotted someone standing in the shadows.

Sparks played around the figure's limbs, surrounding him with living lightning. His skin looked metallic, as though his body were encased in armor. His eyes crackled with electricity.

"Vic!" Ben blurted.

The creature who had been Victor Von Doom stepped forward. "Take a good look, Ben," he said. "This is what a man who embraces his destiny looks like."

He held out his right hand. Electricity streaked down from his shoulders and arced across his fingertips. "I've always wanted power. Now I've got an *unlimited* supply."

A bolt of energy shot from his hand and struck Ben in the chest. Ben flew backward across the room and crashed into a wall. He slumped to the floor, unconscious.

A wicked smile cracked Von Doom's metal face. "One down, three to go," he said.

The lab door flew open, and Reed, fully recovered, dashed inside.

"Right on cue," Von Doom said.

Reed looked from Von Doom to Ben, lying on the floor.

"What did you do?" Reed asked.

"Not me," Von Doom replied, "*you*. You did this to him, Reed—to *all* of us. Now, tell me something: You're the smartest man on earth. What happens when you super-heat rubber?"

He shot energy at Reed, but Mr. Fantastic stretched aside. Von Doom fired again, and this time his blast struck home.

Reed's pliable body flew into the air and crashed

through the window on the far side of the room. Reed stretched and grabbed the side of the building with his rubbery fingers. He slid down the building face, looking something like a human slinky.

Von Doom crossed to the window and watched as his old friend toppled toward the street below.

"Victor!" Sue cried from behind him. "What's happened to you?"

"I'm afraid I'm losing my looks," Von Doom said wryly. "But they say that's less important to a woman than what's inside."

He spun and blasted her with a bolt of energy. The burst slammed Sue back into the wall. Debris rained down on her as the ceiling collapsed, burying her in rubble.

Von Doom strode from the room to the elevators and took the short ride to the lobby.

"Mr. Von Doom," Jimmy the doorman said, "are you okay?"

Victor swatted him aside. "It's *Doctor Doom* now," he said. Jimmy crashed against the wall and slumped to the floor.

Reed's flexible body had saved him from death during his long fall. He lay draped across an awning, melting down the sides like a figure from a surrealist painting.

Doctor Doom grabbed him by the collar. "Come with me," he said. "I'm going to show you what *second place* feels like."

Johnny raced into the shattered remains of Reed's lab. Smoke billowed through the room, making it hard to see. He looked around, stunned by the destruction.

The sound of rubble shifting nearby caught his attention. The faint sound of his sister's voice drifted out of the wreckage.

He helped her dig out of the debris. She looked battered, bruised, and nearly exhausted. "I'm sorry, Sue," he said. "I'm sorry for . . ."

"It's not your fault," she said.

"What happened here?"

"Victor," Sue replied. "He's become something awful. He's taken Reed. We have to do something."

Johnny nodded and said, "Flame on."

He burst into fire, becoming the Human Torch once more.

Doctor Doom paced around his conference room atop the Von Doom Industries tower. The mysterious boxes he'd had delivered loomed behind him. One had been assembled into a hyper-air-conditioning unit. Doctor Doom's breath rolled out in great white clouds into the room's freezing air.

Reed lay on the floor nearby, nearly frozen solid. His breath leaked out in pale gasps.

"Chemistry one-oh-one, part two," Doctor Doom said

to his former friend. "What happens to rubber when it's supercooled?"

Reed struggled to move his lips. "Why don't you . . . kill me?"

"Oh, I will," Doctor Doom said. "But first . . ."

Reed tried to sling his arm at Doctor Doom, but his skin was frozen in place. He couldn't even ball his hand into a fist.

Doctor Doom seized one of Reed's outstretched fingers and bent it back until it cracked. Doctor Doom smiled. "I want you to watch some fireworks," he concluded.

He opened a crate, revealing a rocket launcher. One of the room's huge windows rolled open automatically. Doctor Doom picked up the weapon and stepped onto the parapet outside.

He pointed the rocket launcher toward the Baxter Building and fired.

"Flame off," Doctor Doom said, smiling.

Johnny and Sue heard a sound like thunder. They turned to the window and spotted the missile streaking straight toward them.

"It's locked onto my heat signature," Johnny said.

"Johnny, don't!" Sue said, guessing his next move.

"Sis," he replied, "we're superheroes, not scientists." With that, he leaped out the broken window and burst into flame. The missile arced toward the Human Torch, as Johnny had expected. He concentrated hard, focusing his flame into jetlike force. As he neared the pavement, he began to fly—for real this time. He zipped away from the Baxter Building, talking the missile with him.

Sue watched her brother go and worried. As she gazed out the window, she could see New York's lights flickering—all save for the Von Doom Industries tower, which was lit up like a Christmas tree.

Ben Grimm, the old, human Ben, crawled out of the rubble next to Sue.

Seeing the wreckage, he asked, "What have I done? Where's Reed?"

"Victor's become some kind of monster," Sue told him. "He took Reed."

"We've got to help him," Ben said. He wobbled on his all-too-human legs.

Sue stepped in to support him. "You can't," she said. "Not like you are now. It's too dangerous. Stay here, Ben. Johnny and I will handle Victor."

She helped him to stand and then headed out the door. Ben could only watch her go. He pounded his fist on the wall and hung his head.

Sue was right. Like this, he was helpless.

He walked back into the shattered lab and looked out

the window. Above the city, the Human Torch led Von Doom's missile on an intense chase.

Ben looked over at the transformation machine—still humming with power.

He made a choice.

Johnny blazed across the night sky over Manhattan. He zigged and zagged, using every trick he'd learned in his years as an extreme sportsman. But the missile stayed right with him, its programming adjusting to his every move.

"Not good," Johnny muttered to himself.

Already, he felt tired, but the missile didn't look likely to run out of fuel any time soon.

Reed tried to move, but he couldn't. He could barely breathe. Every molecule of his cosmic storm–altered body seemed frozen. The only thing he could move voluntarily was his eyes. He didn't like what they showed him: Doctor Doom, standing on the balcony, watching a missile chase Johnny across the city.

A quiet footstep sounded near Reed's head. He looked in that direction, but saw nothing. Gradually, Sue faded into view. She held a finger to her transparent lips.

Reed eyes widened, but he couldn't warn her of the danger.

"How romantic," Doctor Doom said from behind her.

Sue turned, shocked at Victor's transformation. He was entirely metal now. All trace of his humanity had vanished.

"Victor," she said, "the chamber worked on Ben, it'll work on you, too. There's still enough energy left for one more transformation. We can turn you back."

Doctor Doom stepped closer to her, electricity playing across his armored skin. He seemed more machine than man.

"Sue, do you really think fate turned us into gods so we could refuse our gifts?" he asked. His voice was cold and metallic.

She stepped away, a force field building around her.

"Sue, please," he said. "Let's not fight."

"No, Victor," she replied. *"Let's."* She hurled her force field at him.

Doctor Doom blasted through it, bursting the energy bubble before it touched him. "Susan," he hissed, "you're fired."

Electricity arced from his hands and struck what remained of Sue's shield. The shock wave launched her through the air. She crashed into the wall and landed next to Reed.

Doctor Doom laughed. "The scientist and his specimen," he said. "The perfect couple. You two always wanted to live together." He raised his hands; they crackled with energy. "Now *die* together."

With one hand, he grabbed Sue by the throat. With the other, he seized Reed's neck and pulled.

Sue desperately shot force bubbles at Doctor Doom, but they burst against his metallic skin.

The lights in the office flickered and dimmed. He smiled and said, "I've been waiting a long time for this."

CHAPTER 18

JOHNNY ROCKETED over the East River, trying to shake the missile from his tail. It was no use. Each second he grew more tired. Each second, the missile drew closer.

He flashed over the water, ducking under bridges and around boats. A garbage barge, unmanned and tied to a dock, loomed ahead of him. Johnny smiled.

He hurled a fireball into it as he zoomed past. The barge caught fire, but the missile was still chasing Johnny. He did a U-turn, and raced back toward the burning barge. The missile crept closer to him.

Just as it was about to hit, Johnny turned off his flame and dived into the water. The rocket streaked past, homing in on the burning barge.

Bang! The missile exploded, blowing the barge to pieces.

Johnny surfaced and pumped his fist in the air. As garbage rained down around him, he swam toward shore.

* * *

In his conference room, Doctor Doom watched the explosion. He smiled, keeping his grip tight on Reed's and Sue's throats.

Reed's neck was stretched impossibly thin, near the breaking point. Sue's eyes fluttered, and she began to fade from view. She and Reed looked at each other, knowing this meant the end. The white clouds of their breath mingled together, one last time.

"And so," Doctor Doom said, "four become *none*. It's my time, now."

"Wrong, Tin Man!" boomed a gruff voice.

Doctor Doom turned as the orange, stone-skinned Thing thundered into the room.

"It's clobberin' time!" Ben bellowed.

Doctor Doom dropped Sue and slammed Reed into the wall, but he couldn't get his guard up in time.

Ben's rocky fist pounded into Doctor Doom's armor, sending him flying across the room and into the wall. The impact shattered the chamber's windows, flooding the conference room with warm air.

Reed looked up, able to move once more.

"That makes six," Ben said to him. "Six times you made me do something I didn't want t—"

Doctor Doom hurled himself into the Thing's rocky body. The two of them smashed through a wall, pulverizing the

133

concrete and shattering windows before hurtling out into thin air.

Ben and Doctor Doom continued their vicious battle as they plummeted toward the earth, many stories below. People on the street screamed as the combatants smashed through the glass roof of the hotel next to Von Doom Towers.

Doctor Doom and Ben plunged into the hotel's huge swimming pool. Terrified swimmers splashed away from the fearsome duo.

As they wrestled underwater, Ben aimed a punch at Doctor Doom's head. Doctor Doom dodged aside and the Thing's fist smashed into the side of the pool. The wall broke, and the pool's water rushed out, carrying both of them with it.

The flood washed onto the street outside the hotel. Ben and Doctor Doom landed inside the back of a large, empty garbage truck.

The two kept swinging. The truck rocked back and forth as they lunged at each other. Every missed punch dented the truck's metal walls. Doctor Doom landed a heavy blow on Ben's face.

The Thing crashed through the back of the truck and landed atop a parked car, crumpling the hood. His rock-like head smashed through the windshield. The two old women inside the car screamed.

Doctor Doom stepped out of the back of the truck.

Ben looked at the old lady behind the wheel. "Excuse me, ma'am," he said. "Can I borrow your car?"

Both women nodded and dived out of the car doors. "The clutch sticks a little," the driver said.

"Not gonna be a problem," Ben replied.

He got up off the hood and grabbed the car with both hands. As Doctor Doom ran toward him, Ben swung the huge car like a baseball bat.

The car slammed hard into Doctor Doom, hurling him through the air. He crashed through a huge glass wall and into a museum. Ben followed him in.

Doctor Doom leaped onto the Thing as he entered, smashing an armored fist into his chest. The Thing flew backward into the street once more. He crashed into a wall, breaking it, and lay stunned in the wreckage.

Doctor Doom grabbed a streetlight. He yanked it from the ground, as though he were pulling weeds in a garden, and crushed it in his fist. Energy from the exposed wires coursed into Doctor Doom's metallic skin. Around him, the lights of New York City dimmed once more.

Clutching the streetlamp, he advanced toward Ben. Electrical energy crackled and sparked across Doctor Doom's metal body.

Ben looked up as Doctor Doom swung the streetlamp at

him. The long metal pole struck the Thing square on the top of the head, knocking him to the ground once more.

Bystanders screamed. Ambulance, fire, and police sirens wailed. News crews moved in, their cameras rolling.

"You might want to get a closeup of this," Doctor Doom said to the reporters. "This is the end of the Fantastic Four."

The Thing staggered to his feet. Doctor Doom kicked him back down.

The streetlight in Doctor Doom's hand glowed as he channeled all his energy into it. He raised it high into the air, aiming to drive the lamppost through Ben's body and into the ground.

CHAPTER 19

BEN LOOKED UP, unable to protect himself from the deadly thrust he was about to receive. Doctor Doom prepared his final blow, but just then the lights flickered on once more. Before it could touch Ben, the pole froze in midair.

Doctor Doom looked aound to see Reed holding the lamp's electrical cords in his outstretched hand. When he turned back, the Thing had disappeared. Unphased Doctor Doom turned and snarled at Reed, standing across the street. "You don't really think you can stop me, all alone!"

Reed smiled fearlessly. "No," he replied. "I *don't*."

Right on cue, Sue turned off her invisibility cloak, revealing Ben and Johnny ready for battle. The three superheroes gathered behind Reed, their leader.

Doctor Doom glanced from Mr. Fantastic to the Thing. "Have you forgotten?" he said to Ben. "This man, Richards, made you what you are—a monster, a freak . . ."

Johnny's eyes narrowed. "I see only one monster here," he said. "And it ain't Ben Grimm."

"That's the *Thing* to you, junior," Ben rumbled.

"This is who we are," Reed said. "*We* can accept it."

"And maybe even . . . ," Sue continued.

"*Enjoy* it," Reed finished.

Doctor Doom leaped at Reed, but Mr. Fantastic was too fast. He stretched his arms with lightning speed, wrapping his enemy in a massive bear hug. Doctor Doom screamed as Reed squeezed him like a python.

"Johnny," Reed said, "supernova!"

Johnny looked at the crowd surrounding them. "But all these people!" he said.

Reed stared into his eyes. "Now!" he commanded. "Do it!"

Reed yanked his arms back, spinning Doctor Doom like a top. Johnny ran toward Doctor Doom, his flames building: first red, then orange, then blazing white-hot. The Human Torch grabbed Doctor Doom's metallic body.

"Flame all the way on!" Johnny cried.

Reed, Sue, and Ben shielded their eyes as Johnny's flame exploded in a pulse of brilliant white light. Waves of scorching heat washed over them.

"Now, Sue!" Reed called. "Concentrate! Now!"

"Susan!" Doctor Doom cried. "No!"

Sue squeezed her eyes shut and focused. A massive force field formed around Doctor Doom and Johnny's supernova blast. The light inside the sphere increased to blinding intensity. Bystanders in the area dived for cover.

The light burned impossibly bright for a few seconds, then faded.

As it did, Johnny collapsed to the sidewalk, exhausted, his body smoking.

Sue slumped to her knees; her force field died away.

Doctor Doom lurched forward, his metallic body glowing white hot. Small drips of molten metal pooled where he stepped.

Sue, Ben, and Johnny gaped at each other.

"Is that the best you can do?" Doom cackled. "You really thought a little heat could stop me?"

Reed faced him, calm and unafraid.

"See, Vic, that's your problem," he said. "You never had much retention. Chem one-oh-one: *last* lesson. What happens when you supercool hot metal?"

In the blink of an eye, Reed whipped his hands toward a fire hydrant across the street. He undid the plug and twined his arms into a fire hose, directing the spurting water at Doctor Doom.

Liquid cascaded from the makeshift hose, crashing into Doctor Doom's fiery metal form. Giant clouds of steam gushed into the air as the villain's body rapidly cooled. Doctor Doom screamed.

"No!"

"You'll excuse me if I savor the moment," Reed said, repeating what Doctor Doom had once told him.

Doctor Doom's screams faded into silence as thick white clouds of mist filled the street, hiding the villain from view.

As the water pressure dropped, Reed unraveled his arms.

The steam rolled back, revealing a frozen metal statue—all that remained of Doctor Doom.

CHAPTER 20

THE FANTASTIC FOUR stood side by side, gazing at the statue that had once been their nemesis. They were battered and bruised, but unbeaten. As one, the quartet smiled.

Cheering New Yorkers poured into the streets. Cars honked their horns, and pedestrians applauded.

"I *love* this job," Johnny said, beaming.

Ben nodded. "I could get used to this."

He hefted the frozen Doctor Doom onto his shoulder and took the metal monstrosity to the lobby of Von Doom Industries. There, he planted it alongside the original statue of Victor. The Thing glanced between the two.

"I don't know," he said. "The new one lacks a certain realism."

Back outside, Reed turned to Sue. She started to say something, but he kissed her. "Sue, don't think. Feel," he said. He looked at her squarely. "Letting you walk out the door was the biggest mistake in my life."

His pliable knees bent down to the sidewalk. His neck stretched up, keeping his face at eye-level with her. His hand scooped up a scrap of metal from the ground. He held it up and Sue could see it was just the size of a ring. Her eyes widened, and she began to vanish.

"I'm not going to make that mistake again. No more variables. Just you. And me," he said.

"So, Sue," Reed said, "will you take me as your . . ."

But she had disappeared completely.

"Sue?" Reed called. "Sue? You there?"

Her finger reappeared inside the ring in his hand. The rest of her returned as she kissed him. "Yes," she whispered.

The crowd cheered.

Ben turned away and looked at the growing mass of people. He was happy for Reed and Sue, but it was hard to see them without thinking about all he had lost. And then he saw her. Alicia was standing in the crowd. He waded through the wreckage to get to her.

"You still looking for that 'three-ton he-man'?" He greeted her.

"Only if it's permanent," Alicia replied.

Just then Reed interrupted them. "Ben, there might be enough particles for one more . . . ," he began. But Ben cut him off. "Forget it, egghead. Sometimes being different isn't such a bad thing."

Then Ben, Alicia, Reed, Sue, and Johnny walked off into a new day in New York City—the dawn of the Fantastic Four.

EPILOGUE

A FEW DAYS LATER, the scene at Von Doom Industries was businesslike. Von Doom's old director of communications, Leonard, was overseeing a group of workers who were loading Doctor Doom's metallic, frozen body into a crate.

Leonard talked into his cell phone as he absentmindedly gazed at what was left of his old boss. Suddenly, a crackle of electricity surged across Doctor Doom's metallic corpse! Leonard's cell phone went to static at the same instant that his jaw dropped at what he had just seen. *Could it be . . .*

An instant later, the heavy lid banged shut over the crate, sealing Doctor Doom in for the journey. An address was stenciled on its face: Latveria.